JEAN-YVES FORTUNY

The Day My Soul Spoke

The most secure door is one that can be left open

Contents

Preface

*'Life is dead
in the memory of the living.'*
Marcus Tullius CICERON

We all knew that in some cases we can surpass our own mental or physical limits. For example, I remember that of a mother – a very small woman. To save the life of her child, she raised the front of a car under which he was stuck.

Is it really superhuman?

Would it be enough for us not to want to make it possible?

She would not necessarily raise the car, but simply save the life of her offspring.
And if we had such a desire in us, are we able to accomplish what we commonly call feats, without being conscious about it?

It was certain that in today's world we sleep…

JYF.

1

Supernatural phenomenon?

'For the ways of the day walk alongside those of the night.'
Homer

I t's three o'clock in the morning. Anselme, a man of seventy nine fell asleep watching a movie in the chair in his living room. He slept deeply.

The television continued to broadcast nightly programs as he entered a phase where dreams and reality merge. His Dog 'Drakkar', a beautiful five year-old husky, slept deeply as well near the his master's chair. Suddenly, crackling came to replace the documentary on the screen, and stealthy flutter of air touched his face, face causing Anselme to change his position.

Drakkar felt something wrong, but did not appear afraid. It only kept one eye open and wagged its tail, sweeping the ground while letting out a little 'woo' which he has the secret.

'Hi, good to see you.' The coat of his skull flattened in an instant.

It looked towards the room, half opening his mouth and let its tongue hang slightly, as if it just swallowed some beef jerky. As a satisfied guest, a face appeared on the screen, whispered something vague, then disappeared. Drakkar got up, went to his master, and licked the inert hand hanging out of the chair 'It's time to go to bed!' then returned to lie on the carpet in front of the door, to sleep peacefully.

Supernatural phenomenon?

Anselme did not knew it, but the journey of his personal evolution was just beginning...

2

Surprise

'Real generosity toward the future lies in giving all to the present.'
André Comte-Sponville

In the Ardèche countryside, in the small village of Saint Just, that a clinic called 'Méribell' was closed recently.

Perched on a hill, the large building had only one fault: its accessibility slowed by the narrowness of the road, upon a protected site. Set upon arches and beams, it majestically overlooks the village and in some ways reminded one of ancient Gallo-Roman architechture. Today restored and refurbished as a hotel of the same name, the old clinic became also a place of pilgrimage for some, with a beautiful garden that encircled the building. But there was something in the air; 'every little thing' that still made the site enjoy the majestic scenery of the past. Moreover, several rooms inside were dedicated to it.

Anselme worked there until his retirement, which he quietly enjoyed in the same village with his wife, Constance.

Truly passionate about his chosen vocation, he took care of the disabled, paraplegic or tetraplegical, and he had many dramatic situations which have certainly profoundly affected him.

As he says, 'Everything was good to live for, even the worst, because we still continue to move forward.'

He knew that better than anyone. He had also found himself disabled during three years after a road accident; but he still managed to get out with an amount of effort. To this day, he still did not knew the significance of that result, which was, according to him a just reward relating to hard work.

Everyone knew him in the village. It was in the eyes of many, he was someone simple and generous even in the medical field. Anselme was part of that generation of nurses who took it easier than many of his colleagues; devoted yet, the little humanity in this world of stress and profitability made him inadequate for these times. Apart for some good advice on the profession, he left former employees with an indelible memory. With a natural kindness, he succeeded in restoring gladness into the heart of his patients who were often broken physically and mentally. His attentive side was appreciated by all and he had even established relationships with some of these people whose life would never be the same before their accidents. But, there was a patient who has left the most impression on him, one he thinks of often. His name was Rémy. He became a quadriplegic after a fifteen-meter drop in his work as a carpenter. Anselme had woven a friendly relationship with him, but as spiritual so to say and when he speaks, it was never without emotion.

On 22 December two thousand and thirteen, he prepared for a day like any other since retiring with Constance. Contrary to the past years they were not entertaining their two children Sébastien and Grégory – they were fathers as well. Both men have planned a trip with their wives and children, in addition to the gifts under the tree, a surprise holidays trip together to 'Disneyland'. They will not be the only ones pleasantly surprised.

In cahoots with Constance, 'Seb and Greg' have received a special invitation for everyone. Anselme did not suspect that he was about to experience the most memorable Christmas in his life.

The clock of the Town Hall showed exactly half past seven; he was about to go dog walking as he did every day. It was the same ritual every morning. Before leaving, he always asks his beloved if he to stop at the supermarket in the village, and over the bakery where he will systematically be going to.

In better times, there was also a stop at the only butcher of the village and the surrounding area. But he had a fault: one in that he wanted to have fun as much as possible. Thus, frequently, it did not bother him to take what he liked, obscuring the need to vary the food and the recommendations of his gentle and loving wife. For him this was really not that big of a default as he can swallow everything except the tripe. But he was what people called a 'free-thinker'. He was convinced that if people continued to tap into nature reserves, there will be a shortage. A theory that he often has to vouch for his calorie-counting wife, Anselme but never thought of it lightly. He inquires, he studies, reads, listens, observes and carefully formulated conclusions that only mattered to him; over the years, however, he became convinced that one day soon, we can certainly eat as much as we liked.

Constance just did not see eye to eye. For her, diversification was essential and, in this regard, Anselme admits readily it was not fundamentally wrong. It took ten years nevertheless for him to consider it, the time of a week-long leave, when her beloved husband was not so refractory to good food, she thought.

They never went on vacation during the first ten years of their marriage, and despite the many opportunities he had balanced meals, he had often managed to escape. But in these past seven days of respite in the mountains in a hostel, there was no choice but to honour the dishes presented to him and it gives her great misfortune. The 'Unfortunate' had to eat only foods that were a part of those that demanded a systematic effort of concentration from him with each gulp. For her part, Constance conceded to the evidence as seen with each swallow without saying anything and sometimes claiming even a second plate!

Before this realization, Anselme, in her eyes, was fussy and she absolutely wanted to change that by any means. So, she did not hesitate to forbid squarely from his 'butcher-stop telling all their friends that he behaved sometimes as a ten-year-old boy. But the information was circulated so that it became the laughing stock of which in his eyes was that of a 'brotherhood of gullible and ignorant people' whose master was none other than his wife as a stubborn ignorant… Of course!

It never, stopped Anselme living the way he wished, but he was with these straight and unequivocal people; he likes to be seen for who he was and not as another character, fabricated and authenticated by others. To him, this type of relationship falsifies everything. Certainly there was no loss of life, but all these little details added to each other unnerved him.

With a saintly patience, at least in general, he held on to some 'rules of life', one of which, of not leaving a situation rot too long, until it was otherwise included in his own life and thus promote cancer! It was true that his views were relatively unusual incited different reactions. But he hated wasting time with problems that did not exist; it will not even be prudent, and he preferred to spend his time on something else. However, when he put himself in poor posture, it was quite capable of taking charge and fixing it, although sometimes a certain time passes before his eyes could take a new look straight ahead.

This radical and unusual behaviour had surprised him; thinking that with time... But Constance had decided to hit the target once and for all; although the fact of seeing her husband react just to make her happy and have peace, had the gift of testing her patience.

Left to his devices, Anselme heads towards the entrance where Drakkar waited for him, so as to attach it to its harness – he had preferred it to the collar. Not knowing what Constance planned for meals this festive day before year's end, he preferred to confirm.

'Are you preparing something special this year?'

'No, don't bring anything in today, I have a surprise for you with the children, but I have been sworn to silence. Let yourself go and all will be well!'

This was all Constance's style to say things without saying them. Anselme smiled and did not seek further.

'With the children. Why, are they coming?'

'Maybe, maybe not!'

'Well I will not insist; would it thwart your plans if I go out and walk the dog?'

'Go away!' replied Constance, amused!

The simple act of taking its leash had the dog in all sorts and stretched his 'woo' for a few seconds, as if rolling an 'R' as wolves did. It hopped about as if a trampoline was grafted onto each of its legs. Anselme knew and was amused. He purposely made it wait until it started barking.

In its language, there was no doubt, he was being sermoned. 'Get that leash on me already and let's go!'

In Saint-Just, as in many small countrysides, the leash was not necessarily required. But he soon realized that it was better to have a means of control to curb the power of the animal when it encounters people in the village streets. Not making the difference between a bipedal and sled, it had already happened to Anselme to be 'dragged' as such or again, toppling people backwards by standing on its two hind legs, two forelegs themselves being posed with some momentum on their chest.

'Come boy, quickly.'

Drakkar, who has already made covered a kilometre in place, cannot be held back. Their neighbour, Bernard, was already 'in place'; the man rises early at seven in the morning and takes pleasure in waiting, sipping coffee on the terrace in front of the house when the weather allows it.

'Hi Nanar!'

'Good morning Anselme. What a wonderful day ahead. It'll be a pleasure to garden today.'

'And what are you going to garden with this freezing cold?'

At that time, Drakkar barked twice…

'No hellos for me?'; it made the two men smile. Bernard came and gave the dog a pat.

Anselme took the opportunity to try to learn more about the surprise that awaited him as they had excellent neighbourly relations, and did not have many secrets from one another. But Bernard was forced to give his speech. Sure, it looks like nothing.

'So that's how you treat a friend?

'Sorry Anselme, you knew your wife better than me and I want to stay alive!

'You're a traitor!

'Yes pal, I know, and that's why we've always been friends!'

There was absolutely nothing to do, he will not knew ahead of time.

He conceded, and went off to walk his sled-puller of a dog. Along the way, he encountered people he usually crossed paths with; they exchange a few words, a few small talk. Without forgetting the daily pilgrimage in which he never failed to make the outskirts of the old clinic that reminded him so much of good times.

But today was a special day, one that heralded a great event, a 'key' moment in his life. Within a few minutes, he took to thinking of the patient, 'Rémy' that fate had placed in his way. He was the one with whom he had sealed this special friendship; him who imposed on himself a 'relationship code' with the people he took care of, which consisted of not to be personally invested, had eventually succumbed to the magic of the same wavelength on which they themselves on. This relationship that bordered friendship and fraternity had nothing in common with what he had experienced before. It was forged over the days, months and years during which it had developed in such a beautiful way that might suggest to those who have neither brother or sister, and that there was in this world at least one person whom we want to hope for, from whom we won't conceal our true selves, feel good about ourselves without a second thought.

With his eyes on the building, despite himself, he let a tear fall, as he was invaded by a moment of sadness. Images jostling in his mind, he relived some of his memories, extraordinary moments he spent in the rooms he visited often, and more often than not, that of Rémy's...

'Hello Rémy, did you sleep well?'

'No, I was in the dumps and I had to sleep at two or three in the morning.'

'You want to talk about it? Well, I mean...'

'Okay, I understand. You just need time to adapt, that's all.'

'That's true, I still can't believe I'm doing this...'

9

'You've been able to identify the first sign; I made it into your head... Well not just yet!'

'What's this "not just yet"? What do you mean?'

'Just as you're about to discover yourself and if you work well, you will eventually knew yourself...'

'Look, I have no desire to philosophize today, so make it simple.'

'You are not feeling well, it's obvious.'

'You noticed it yourself?'

'Non Anselme, you helped me...'

'Rémy, I beg of you, not now.'

'It really is just you who hold me down here.'

'Don't do that! What about the others then?'

'You knew very well what I mean; I will not hold like this forever. I love you like a brother Anselme. You knew how to open your heart and you knew very well that this isn't the kind of thing we do with just anyone. You managed to give me a reason to hold on to life. I love all of our conversations, our debates, our jokes, our extrapolations. I never shared this with anyone before knowing you. I have often thought of everything I could share with a brother and I cannot help but be drawn to you. What you've given me is priceless. I am really happy to have you and I knew I will be forever grateful, but I'm tired of lying on that bed all day. I can come up with all the mental coping mechanisms, but I can't, for the life of me, move a single limb, and you've became my only source of communication in this world. I've lost faith Anselme, I don't want to live like this anymore...'

'Don't expect me to...'

'I know, I'm a big boy; I won't burden your conscience like that.'

At that time, Anselme felt his arms tremble and put the equipment he held in his hands on the table, unable to control his emotions.

'You're telling me you don't want to live?'

'I knew you understand. I'm tempted to say you're even letting your ego show!'

'How can you say such a thing?

'You know… you too I will miss you, but I knew I will miss you more once I'm over there.'

'Over there…

'In that place where I can live again…'

'You have good ones, you know,' Anselme replied with a bitter smile, trying to hide deep distress!

'We already talked about it some time ago, remember?'

'Of course… but…'

'You don't want to have to mourn my death, that's your problem!'

Anselme could not control himself and spoke aloud. 'Enough! How can you knew how I feel!'

In anger, he picked up his 'tools' and went out, slamming the door.

'Wait, Anselme, my friend…'

'Save it for later!'

This was not the first time that his colleagues saw him out of that room as if annoyed with himself. They divined an unusual situation, even in some strange ways, but they respected the man in front of their eyes and had the decency not to ask any questions. In those cases, he would take refuge in the coffee break room and try to drink between sobs. He regretted being carried away. He did not see this time that the behaviour he had with that with Rémy was that of a kin. He understood Rémy, but he was unable to stand losing a loved one. What should come first? My wish, or his? The answer was obvious, but it was so hard not to be able to talk anymore, joke or argue with people who show us their best sides. All these thoughts haunted his mind often, and the feeling of missing something important weighed heavily on him. With a tear in the eye, Anselme remained for a few more seconds in front the building.

'I miss you, and I blame you for leaving when you could have lived. You had the ability, you who did it in thought; but you preferred to let me down, to leave me alone here with my grief.'

Feeling alone frequently happened to him in those moments. Fortunately, there was in the world around him; namely in his family who allowed him to continue to love, but those were other feelings – certainly pleasant, but which were not dedicated to Rémy. Although he has around him Bernard, his neighbour, as friend he cannot help thinking that he'll never experience that again with someone else. But what made him bitter was mainly the fact that he never accepted the death, like a disease that eats you from the inside and prevents you from living your life.

Seeing him like that, Drakkar got up on its hind legs, leaned against him, and licked his face. Perhaps it meant that it will let him down, perhaps it said simply 'I'm here for you, I love you.'

Wiping his tears, Anselme takes the way back.

'You're a good dog "Drakky."'

Something suddenly grabbed the dog's attention, and it remained frozen in pace letting out its 'sample bark,' 'Woo'.

'Well, buddy, what do you got?'

Drakkar started again on all fours and barked twice, looking at Anselme's side as if someone was standing beside him. Anselme looked in turn, but only saw a deserted street. 'Hey, you'll have to tell me! After you've barked like that? Don't you become senile before me! Come on, let's go home.'

Meanwhile, a bit of the surprise had come home in the form of two large spacious cars in which were his two sons, two daughters-in-law, and three grandchildren. Constance had secretly prepared two suitcases took advantage of Anselme's absence to load them in one of the spacious trunks.

'Hello, children, did you have a good trip?'

'Yes, there weren't many people at that hour. Hello, mother. And you have prepared everything on your end?'

'Yes, and your father doesn't suspect a thing.'

'He was with Drakkar?'

'Yes, he shouldn't be long. Want to drink coffee in the meantime?'

'I'll never say "no", mother. I love your coffee!'

'Hello Sofia, hello Véronique, hello little ones.'

Constance welcomed everyone with happiness and love. Upon his return, Anselme quickly hurdled the steps that he missed. He strictly knew nothing, but upon entering the house, he did not resist the urge to show them 'that nothing surprised him.

'So where were we going?'

His reaction did not surprise anyone save for the two beautiful girls who did not knew him well. Anselme did not know what to expect, but he knew well that they did not conspire to share his life insurance. He decided to be guided to the end, somewhat impatient and looking forward to see where it will lead him. Constance took the lead.

'You like the cartoons with 'Mickey', right? Well, that's where we're going!'

'You want to see me as a child again!'

'Why not?' approved Constance, 'But most importantly is that there are a lot of other people in this world who think of you...'

'Excuse me?'

Anselme frowned. He looked towards Constance who made her way to the kitchen, leaving him standing there, cat catching his tongue.

'But... dear, who you mean?'

He knew she enjoyed playing that game. The knowing her, he did not insist.

'Okay, enough mysteries, let's go!'

The day stared well. Everything seemed to unfold perfectly. Anselme was in excellent mood, the children were happy to be there, and Constance was deeply convinced that those holidays were unforgettable.

All had a vague idea about how Anselme was going to spend the evening Greg and Seb exchanged a knowing glance with their mother who was very excited to see what happened to the man she loves. Aside from tensions that stood between Grégory and his father some time ago, there was no way to ruin the holidays with the past.

Everyone sat around the dining room table to enjoy a good breakfast. The slogan was 'mum's the word' in respect of Anselme. But they should not overdo it because they would have ended up making things uncomfortable.

Coming back from the kitchen with his hands in a tray packed with coffee, cups and milk, Constance clarified that they could not take the dog to Paris.

'We'll just leave it with Bernard, they both love each other,' Anselme replied calmly!

Realizing that she had omitted the sugar on the kitchen table, she rose, followed by Sophia, a little intrigued.

'Yes Sofia what's the matter?'

'Can I ask you a somewhat delicate question?'

'If it's not too much so, yes!'

'Is he always like that?'

'Like what?'

'Well, he did not know what was waiting for him, and I just see him accept something that would mess up his plans with such serenity!'

'You know, Anselme was someone who takes life as it comes. If you ask him, he will tell you that life was made so, that is, full of spontaneity.'

'Yes, but with this, he discovers that he will have to endure a 1400-kilometer round trip to an unknown place, where he doesn't knew what to expect! Many don't take it as well as he does.'

'He doesn't care,' said Constance. 'Surprises don't bother him. He knew well enough that were cooking up something for him. Also, I never gave him reason to be suspicious of me.'

'That's a good thing when mutual trust remains strong in a couple. That was what we strive to do, Greg and I.'

'And you well to stick to that essential rule,' assured Constance. 'I never had that problem with Anselme. He has a trustful nature. Besides, we've already argued about it.'

'Oh, really?'

'I blamed him for being too naive in the past. He confided in everyone, always unsuspecting, and it just drove me up the wall!'

'That doesn't sound so bad though,' said Sofia, 'it's rather nice to be capable of giving yourself so easily, even if it happens that some are not worthy.'

'You're absolutely right Sofia. It was precisely how he changed me. Before meeting him, I also did not give as easily as that, you know. I often felt the need to put people to the test as soon as the opportunity arose. But I over time I realized that we only get reactions to the provocations we do.'

'I understand. It's more a question of human relations, right?'

'Exactly. For him, one must be able to trust his environment.

He often says, "It's always one less worry." All his life is based on that philosophy. You apparently have a lot to learn. But I knew how to observe him, and he taught me a lot about life. Anselme is someone who lives day by day while being able to look into the future much more than all of us together.'

'There's such a difference with my father. If anything changes in his daily organization, he was lost!'

'He should probably be scared. But only he knows the answer to that question. We all have a burden on our shoulders. And your father-in-law has always fought to eliminate problems before they become a burden. It's not obvious but when observed, you wonder if we live on the same planet as he does. Yet, he's like you and me. Only his life philosophy makes a difference. If you wish, we can resume that talk another time. In the meantime, know that he also has his own damn faults, but you don't scream it out too loud, right?'

'Right. I must admit that since I've lived with Greg, I ask myself about it more and more because he inherited that behavior. Discussing it with you will probably help me to better understand him, sometimes.'

'We'll talk about it, I promise.'

'Thank you, Constance.'

'Don't mention it. At the same time, I'm investing on my son's happiness,' she joked smirking. 'Shall we, then? Here, bring the sugar.'

Greg had understood that they had a conversation.

'Is everything alright, sweetie?'

'Yes. Here's the "coffee softener"!'

Sofia took her place beside her husband and Constance joined in'.

'Well, you have the choice between chocolate croissants and

16

croissants. They're from yesterday, but they should be swallowed easily.' Constance specified.

'It doesn't matter if that's the case, your coffee will make up for it.' Sébastien assured her!

'Thank you for the compliment my son. Go on, we shouldn't delay, attack and bon appétit to everyone! We have at least a seven-hour drive ahead.'

As soon as they were finished, Anselme rose from the table and took Drakkar to Bernard's.

'Ah, so it's now that you bring him to me!'

'Needless to tell you all the time it took, but I guess you already know!'

'Do you think you could forgive me by the time we turn eighty?'

'I'll think about it during the trip. You know what to do with the dog, right? Look, it's just if he's not pushing me to I go away!'

'Don't worry. Now scram, and Merry Christmas to you all!'

'To you too and thank you. Hug Suzanne for us, and above all, behave yourselves!'

Bernard knew part of what was waiting for his friend. He looked at him head back to his house and could not help but reveal an admiring smile.

'You see, Drakkar, I'll tell you something very important.' He crouched at the height of the animal's snout, he stroked its head and looked into its eyes.

'Never change masters!'

Drakkar licked his face. It certainly was his way of telling him 'It will never happen!'

His wife Suzanne, never rises before nine in the morning. Like Bernard, she knew their friend's project and was not surprised to find her husband in the company of Drakkar, all settled on the terrace. Eyes still half closed, she came with two cups of coffee in hand.

'Hello "Panou"'. That was the inherited nickname from former generations of Italians she gave him. She planted a kiss on his cheek and settled in with them.

'So where are they?

'They're preparing and shouldn't delay in getting started.'

'Anselme still knows nothing?'

'No, it will really be a surprise.'

'It's beautiful what's happening to him, do not you think?'

'Not for someone like him dear, I would say that it's normal. And as far as I know it was well deserved.'

'You're right, he's a good person.

'It can't be otherwise since he's our friend… our best vehicle!'

It became a joke between them. With time, they had come to subscribe to the 'Anselme philosophy' which was a definition of a rather personal friendship…

'A friendly or romantic relationship can be compared to a car today. Sometimes a piece messes up; all you have to do is to just repair to keep on moving forward, even if sometimes, it costs you something. Like cars, any relationship grows either way. It already starts with the choice. Then, we supply with fuel, and we don't give him diesel if he would rather the premium; we must respect his tastes. We clean up when we're dirty; we respect the mechanics for not rushing and therefore cause a strong reaction with it; we make trips. Sometimes he can be whimsical and can exasperate us to the point of us swearing against it. But those are only temporary, everyone has his character…'

'Oh, here they come, 'said Suzanne.

She raised an arm to greet them. Anselme and his family did the same. They boarded the two great cars and slowly began their journey by making a last wave to their friends. Drakkar jumped up and followed them along the enclosure to the end of the field barking, 'I'll miss you...'

There were not gone for ten minutes that the post man arrived on his bike to drop a letter in their mailbox.

'Hello Daniel, you just narrowly missed, they just left!'

'Hello you two, hello Drakkar. There's nothing for you today.'

'That's just fine,' says Suzanne, 'you can keep the bills!'

'I'd take the message, but if they put as much time to arrive as that the letter addressed to Anselme, you'd be at peace for the next fifteen years!'

'Oh, why so?' questioned Bernard.

'Because it was sent in nineteen-ninety-four! I'll head out, I'm late, good day.'

Bernard and Suzanne looked intrigued.

'Hopefully we will not get them all at the same time in nineteen years,' he continued to grunt!

'Bernard, we would almost be ninety years old,' can you imagine!

She looked to the distance, hoping to see the convoy that was already kilometers away, and continued,

'You must realize that it's all very strange...'

'How it can happen; what do you think? And if it was an important news, we already are in thousand and thirteen! I do not know, it's definitely a Christmas filled with mysteries this year.'

3

On the way!

'Happiness is something that multiplies when divided.'
Lao-Tzu

Sébastien and Grégory were the two drivers. Respectively twenty-five and twenty-six years old, they got their driver's license together and were still in the period where seven hundred kilometres to cover wasn't a problem. Constance chose to ride with Grégory, and Anselme with Sébastien.

Sofia was delighted with that choice as she loved her mother-in-law. About Anselme, either with one or the other, it did not matter. His relationships with his two sons were different, sometimes explosive in the past, but they were good. The largest difference between the two lay in Sébastien's sensitivity, which was more pronounced. Settled at the front of the car, Anselme started the conversation.

'Son, I must admit that I have a preference for the music you listen to. You still love Celtic music?'

'Oh yes, more than ever! Check out that CD...'

Anselme carefully scrutinized most of the tracks he knew.

'Well, the trip promises to be nice,' he continued, 'Carlos Núñez, Al Braz Dan, Rita Connolly, Gilles Servat, you spoil us.'

20

'Véronique, and you, do you like that music?'

'Yes, I love it! For me, it's like classical music but a little more upbeat, made out of ordinary instruments.'

'You probably mean the bagpipes?'

'Yes, among others. And there are also those chants. They are simply beautiful.'

'Those by Denez Prigent for example, are very beautiful.'

'Tell me, children. When do you intend to tell me what to expect?'

'Well, not today, Dad!'

'Véronique, if I entrusted a secret on Sébastien, would you tell me?'

At that time, he cast a furtive glance at his amused son and grandchildren, reassuring them with a wink. But the judgment soon began to fall!

'Oh grandpa, what a cheater!'

'And you my dear little son whom I love…'

'Forget it grandpa!'

'You're no better than my friend Bernard,' he joked!

Sébastien smiled. But Véronique decided to turn the tables around.

'I can tell you a little more if you want!'

Surprised, the children watched their mother anxiously.

'There is at least an understanding person in this car! I'm listening; I can reward you for your action!'

Sébastien knew very well that she would not say anything, and looked forward to the silliness that went through her head.

'Well, "Grandfather dear," I can tell you that that will be at the Christmas of a lifetime, as far as I know…!'

Anselme waited a few moments before responding.

'And that's it…?

'Yes, Anselme; but admit that reply is worth well against your attempt at finding us out!'

'Your wife has a lot of humor, Sébastien' said 'grandpa', a little disappointed, but pleased to see a character 'worthy of his son' in his daughter-in-law!

'Well, joking aside, he continued. I will stop teasing you and get some sleep. See you later, children.

Respectful, Sébastien lowered the volume of the music. From that moment, everyone was careful not to make noise.

'I'll make you happy dad; so you can sleep all soundly, I present to you this Celtic music concert as a 'canvas' for your dreams. You'll tell me all about it.'

Véronique watched with amusement, Anselme replied, 'Now here's someone who has a heart in this family!'

But Véronique was not one to be outdone...

'Yes, I know,' says the young woman coolly, in an ironic tone!

Anselme smiled, then took a more comfortable position and fell asleep over the miles. The children took the same path. Soon, only Véronique and Sébastien were the only two people awake in the large family.

Véronique took the opportunity to ask her husband on that famous invitation to learn more.

'You knew the people who sent us that invitation?

Sébastien did not answer right away, and preferred to first make sure that his father slept soundly enough to not hear their conversations.

'Nothing was said about two million Euros we must pay for the accident, alright!'

Véronique rolled her eyes, but quickly realized that it was a way like any other to make his father react in case he stirred. He knew that hearing something was alarming, he would have worried

22

and asked for an explanation.

'Okay, we can talk,' said Sébastien!

'Are you sure he's sleeping?'

'Yes, don't worry, he still asleep like a log.'

Casting a glance at her father-in-law, Véronique continued.

'For a brief moment, I believed you. You were toeing the line!'

'At least we're sure that he's sleeping. Going back to the invitation, I knew the people who sent it to us.'

'Oh, so, who are they?'

'I don't know them personally, but I've heard a lot in my childhood. If I remember correctly, it was dad's colleagues who wanted to surprise him.'

'That's really nice! What was that surprise?'

'They didn't spread it around. It looked to be an evening in which the guest of honour will be my father. But I was surprised to see that it happened in Paris, because in my memory, if it was the persons whom I'm thinking about, they all live in Saint-Just or just around the area.'

'Maybe they wanted to make it big,' ventured Véronique!

'It's possible. In any case, they didn't lay out the details. But anyway, it coincides with our project for the children; we won't be far away.'

'Yes, that way we'll already be there. There's still a detail that escapes me. It's not for his name-day or for his birthday?'

'No, not yet, obviously, it's for Christmas time that they decided to organize it. I think they must have their reasons.'

'I think it's too much trouble though; why are there so many mysteries around that evening?'

'To tell you the truth, I don't know, they might've expected something special and want to make it a complete surprise.'

'You're probably right; they must have the means to take care of our rooms, because there's ten of us, it's not nothing.'

'If they can, then they can afford it and should greatly appreciate it.'

'You surprise me! You can't just do it like that. I like your father too, I think he's cool.'

'It's true that with age, he's softened, but he wasn't always with the flow, you know!'

'Yes I can see it. He must've been an unworthy father, looking at you!'

Sébastien bowed his head for a moment, picking up on the joke.

'It was hell, we were very unhappy…'

'One could almost believe it, darling!'

'Really?'

He let a few moments go by, then resumed.

'I may have missed my calling as a film actor,' he said, smiling!

'Well then… it doesn't tell me he's a bad father!'

'I meant it was harder before, strict, if you prefer. For instance, when Grégory or I messed up, we were entitled to a long punishment to start us off which eventually lead to a spanking. If it was important and amounted to certain amount of money to pay off, he arranged it so that we would do some work or that we'd work for the complainant until we made up for the loss. It was true that at the time it wasn't very cool, but looking back, even if we found it hard, he wasn't an awful father; in his way, he taught us values, good manners and especially how to be responsible for our actions. And when my mother saw that he was going too far, she intervened and reasoned with him.

'Your mother also seems to have his character,' emphasized Véronique. 'I love talking to her, we have very interesting conversations.'

'She's even more so now, because she shares in things. She was

24

as nice as you see her today, but her psychology drove us crazy. She managed to even crack my father a few times!'

'Hers psychology you say?'

'To summarize in a few words, when she started to analyze a situation, it could take two hours. And just to avoid that, we had to be extra careful in all that was said. But you must recognize that was often right!'

'She was a psychologist in the past?'

'No, but I realized later that it came from her childhood.'

'Oh, she was unhappy?'

'There was a bit of that, yes. She was rejected in her childhood, and she started very early to analyze situations, people, because she trusted no one.'

'That'd be normal...'

'All that, I understood in time and when I talk to her today, it's different, I hear her with a different ear... Even when she points out that an actor hadn't closed his car door properly in a movie!'

Véronique smiled.

'Don't you want to sleep for a bit?' asked Sébastien.

'Maybe; I'll lie down on the seat and I'll see later.'

'Whatever you want sweetie.'

There was still a question nagging Véronique for a while; 'It's a good opportunity to talk about' kind of thought. She wanted to get to the bottom of it.

'Love...'

'Yes...' *She'll be dead tired if she doesn't close her eyes a bit*, he thought.

'I overheard a conversation two months ago between when your parents over our last visit, they spoke of a certain Rémy and your father looked upset; was he his brother?

Sébastien had heard about him for a long part of his childhood,

Rémy became at one time the main subject of conversations during meals. He had also felt some jealousy about it.

'No, they weren't brothers, at least not in this life...'

'What do you mean?'

'Rémy was one of his patients at Méribell, and in other circumstances, they would have been the best of friends, even though it was... already more or less the case, but he was a quadriplegic. All I can tell you was that he loved him like a brother, because my father was his only family. Sleep now, you need some sleep.'

Véronique no longer insisted on the matter. She lay back in her seat, but had a hard time getting to sleep.

In the preceded them, the atmosphere was joyful. Gérémi, Grégory and Sofia's only son, enjoyed making signs to the car behind them. He squirmed, but he knew Sofia he would calm down quickly.

'Apparently Kévin and Angel have already fallen asleep, and it looked like Véronique will do the same,' remarked Constance!

'Probably,' said Sofia, 'their two toddlers are much more calm than Gérémi. But overall, we don't have much to complain about.'

The convoy soon arrived on the motorway towards Paris. Those who were sleeping were definitely in Morpheus' arms. Both drivers had perhaps not many years of driving behind them, but they evolved to a constant speed with great flexibility.

4

Dreams or nightmares?

'The body and soul are not two different entities,
but two ways of understanding the same thing.'
George Santayana

A nselme was fast asleep and not snoring, contrary to the usual. One could make out a smile on his face. He looked really happy, he dreamed. But that dream was unusual, as if he were being duped, as if someone had interfered in his head.

He went several years back; he found himself in nineteen-ninety-two. It was the time when he was a nurse in the 'Méribell' clinic. Everything was just like he remembered. But something was off. He had the feeling that he knew someone at that time, and had come to take him by the hand just to take him there, with a specific objective in mind.

He suddenly saw a human form surrounded by a thin white aura, similar to a bright armor providing foolproof protection. He could not make out their face, but he had the feeling he knew them; that luminous being approached more toward him, gently but surely, until he could make out their clearer lines. 'No, that's not possible, I must be dreaming!' Anselme thought, distraught.

'The Being' was only a few steps from him and continued to advance calmly. Their face finally appeared to him; and a broad smile spread on Anselme's face who tried to control but whose expression betrayed deep emotion.

'Rémy, it's you... It really is you?'

Anselme was so moved that he could not help but shed a tear, as his emotions were so strong.

'Anselme, my friend, I'm glad to see you.'

Rémy smiled and was just as happy.

'How was this possible; Am I dead?'

'Absolutely not! But I've always said that everything was possible with the mind: just believe. And then, you're just dreaming!'

'You cannot imagine how happy I am to see you. The day shen you died, it was as if a part of me had gone.'

'That's how it happens between two friends,' Rémy told him, putting a hand on his shoulder.

'Your winking, I really missed it, you know.'

It was the means of communication they had established when they were not alone. A blink meant 'yes' and two meant 'no.'

'As have I, it was your presence that I missed most. But I never was far either.'

'How so?'

'I'll explain it all later. For now, come with me. There's something you don't know and that you have to see.'

'Where are you taking me?

'Here in Méribell, but at the time, the advice that you've given them, eventually bear fruit. You believed that you were talking to walls with each of them and they were able to make you believe that.'

'What were you talking about?'

'Remember...'

'How do you... you mean to say that...'

'Yes Anselme, I mean it! And after that, everything changed at Méribell; all eventually left for their home as you know. They have so much respect for you, they wanted to show you the fruits of their work because it was not always easy for them.'

'Yes, no doubt about it.'

Suddenly Anselme had a surprise.

'Since we're taking, I just realize that you're standing up and I speak with you as we have never been able to do before. But it's true that I shouldn't be surprised around you!'

'I cannot possibly explain everything Anselme. All I can tell you is that we'll meet again one day; but if I tell you too much, I'm afraid that you'd to want to join me before your own time!'

'So if I'm understanding what's happening, you'll make use of telepathy or something to create all this?'

'Non Anselme, you simply travelling in space-time!'

'What?'

Rémy could not help laughing.

'Yes my friend, we were really in nineteen-ninety-two!'

'But how do you do that?'

'The spirit, Anselme, always and forever with the spirit... Remember all those conversations we had on that subject; remember the first time we communicated with our minds.'

'It was true that before I met you, I would never have thought myself capable of doing such a feat.'

'You used the right word; it was a feat in question, and not a gift.'

'Yes I remember your explanations; we do not even use ten percent of our abilities, and when someone says to have a gift of spirit travel or telekinesis or I do not knew what else, we talk

29

about supernatural when it was really just nothing, that's it… I'm not mistaken, right?'

'That's exactly right! But you could have chosen something simpler: for example, when a person makes a premonitory dream, we are certainly not in the supernatural because that's how we usually look at it, but if we look a little closer, it's already a first step towards clairvoyance, so those are one of the feats that we do not use often… consciously, anyway.' said Rémy, who was in a better position to address the issue.

'And can you tell me how you actually do it?'

'You had talked to me one day about your childhood, of those nocturnal escapades you were doing with your seven-league boots, do you remember?'

'As if it were yesterday; I loved that cartoon and it's true that I can still feel it today, nearly sixty years later. How I rose from the room and stepped over the rooftops, four by four. I often went to the Tarascon Castle, since that's where we lived. It was really a unique sensation. In those moments, I was so light in such serenity and I felt such freedom, that I thought that I no longer wanted to go home… And I was only four years old!'

Anselme stopped dead and then continued,

'I understand; I think I know the answer to the question.'

'Well for me, it's quite the same principle; the only difference, is that my body's dead, and that's the only way I have that I can move. To top it off, I can even make it through time!'

'You have all the answers, if I could do what I did when I was a kid, I imagine it must be possible to do it at any age.'

'In theory yes, we can do everything, but the one who decides to develop such capacity, or if you prefer to explore ninety percent dormant of your dormant capacities, you would quickly be regarded as an alien or as someone who has a one-way ticket to the asylum, because we have all our capabilities awakened at birth. But we lose them as we grow up, no thanks to our environment. Nobody could ever understand; those who could probably to do so shut themselves down because others fear them. A bit like the "high-level autistics" who are capable of what we believe to be true prowess, but in fact they just focus on what they do, where their talents are put into practice. For us, they are in that we call "a world apart" but if everyone around them gave way to explore one or more capabilities without cutting them off from the world, they would be so-called "normal" people. The world as it was today is not ready to receive so much information in one go; it will happen, but little by little, news item after news item, like the man who developed his sight without even noticing because he was slow to remove a plug of wax in his ears!'

'Really?

'Yes; he simply switched the sense of vision which offered new features: colours considerably exacerbated, a far superior vision, more accurate, more efficient and revealing. He had consciously managed to put his finger on the process, which was generally developed in cases of extreme emergency. All come with time, of that I'm sure.'

'How can you be so sure?'

'It's because I've been there!'

5

Spiritual walk

'The beginning of all sciences,
is the surprise that things are what they are.'
Indira Gandhi

'Y ou've been there... but where?'
'I visited the future, I went up to the year two thousand two hundred!'
The two friends often philosophized about the future of our civilization. Anselme sometimes spent two or three hours after his shift when his physical state permitted. But it was not their single favourite subject. Their telepathic conversations covered all sorts of current news, the Steven Spielberg film, sometimes about some gossip in the clinic. Each in turn philosopher, journalist, or any gossip like any two friends, Anselme greatly appreciated those moments. He shared them with no one but him. As for Rémy, he lived just what he had never known before.
'In two thousand two hundred! And what did you see?'
'I can tell you that everything has changed dramatically. People were in a completely different mindset. Even God took a beating!'
'God,' says Anselme taken aback? And what happened to him, a blackout in heaven?'

'Be serious for a minute; people discovered that "God" was no more or no less than qualifier... The part of the Bible carefully hidden by the Vatican stating that "God is in us, God is everywhere around us, not in churches of stone and wood" has been brought to light for a long time. Everything was explained in the long and the short. More than a hundred and twenty years before the world completely accepted it. That means that "God" is us, or rather all of us, on top of what we can do or can be or to simplify, to be the best of ourselves.'

'You're saying that "God" was simply a word?'

'Yes, exactly; in other words, we were all gods in power! Besides, if you think about it, the one who believes in him does not need to believe in anyone else. When we say 'thank you God,' we thank him for what? His wave of a magic wand? It's still the man, and he alone, who takes care of his problems, not a legendary entity perched on a cloud!'

'Somehow, what you're saying there makes sense. But why tell me in this case? It seems to me that I am part of all these people, even if I am a little more open-minded and I'll meet you in many ways,' says Anselme amazed.

'Because it was you who will be the forerunner of a new era in your field. In the future, the whole world will know you for all that you did for them. You knew how to press the right "switch". You have changed their lives, and you became for medicine and life itself as to what Einstein was to science. It all started with you!'

'Really?'

'Yes Anselme, but I assure you, when you wake up completely later, you won't remember nothing.'

'Why?'

'It's not hard to imagine! You will begin to understand much

33

earlier than you think.'

'And there's another one! Right now everyone around me's conspiring not tell me anything!'

'You think that I haven't revealed anything to you today?'

'It's true that you told me, but won't remember, then!'

'Now pull yourself together a bit and follow me, I'll show you what you did.'

'But... but... what's happening...? It feels like I'm flying!'

Rémy looked Anselme with a big smile.

'There's a bit of that. Here's the place... We're now in two thousand and two!

'In two thousand and two?'

Anselme suddenly felt being watched...

'Look out,' he said, suddenly.

'Don't worry, no one can see us. The most sensitive may be able to guess at our presence, but that's it.'

'Wait a minute... I recognize them!

'Of course, you worked with them,' said Rémy.

'But what are they doing?'

'You can see it!'

'I cannot believe it.'

'And you, what have you done? You did well out in your own way!'

'That's true...'

'And how have you succeeded, you remember, right?'

Those simple words plunged Anselme a few years back. He began, without realizing it, to walk the road to deliverance...

'Several factors are in play. I've often 'filmed' my life in difficult times. Music helped me a lot. I could feel the vibrations to the depths of my being and the emotion it held. It was as if my life became a movie in which I had the lead role. I imagined

Constance and all the people I love sitting in front of a movie screen after all my efforts moved me forward as you would with the hero of the story. I did not only for me but also for them.

'I documented myself, a long time ago, the reaction of animals to different sounds. Most react with ultrasound and infrasound, like at our birth, but we lose that capacity growing up. Whoever wanted to prevent an earthquake on a seismic zone, has to place a natural reserve with animals of all species. The day we see the panic and want to leave, you can be one hundred percent sure that a disaster was imminent. We can therefore conclude that they react to that, they might respond to other sounds, if they are treated as sentient beings. Moreover, I think research was done on the subject. Well it's the same for us. The only difference between them and us was our evolution, our way of life. And that we reacted to other sounds.'

'You're a real source of science, Anselme.' joked Rémy, 'but it's true that you never stopped with just medical books!'

'And you knew something, huh?', Anselme joked in turn, 'but it's not just that, there was also the crystal... You know about the crystal...?'

'If you had asked me that in my lifetime I would have said that you I had heard about it, but now it's different, I had the opportunity to see it...'

'Oh yes! And at what time did you go to see how to use that rock?'

'That was long before our civilization, long before our era!'

'It's amazing that, if we could see everything that you see in our lifetime!'

'No Anselme, you will lose all your landmarks... Think for thirty seconds... Even I found it hard to return.'

'Why, it's too far?

'In a way, yes. It was simply not part of our era. But we're starting to get lost there, you spoke of the crystal...'

'Yes, to return to the sounds that make us react, the crystal, in my point of view, what there was of better. I want to specifically mention crystal bowls, which were sound rotators that awaken our awareness and encourage us to reflect on ourselves and on our relationship with the world. The sound immediately puts us in harmony with our "inner selves" because it's precisely there where we seem to come from. It awakens our thinking and our thoughts are stimulated, revealing our dormant qualities and hidden talents. All in all, it develops our potential. The effect of the resonance in our bodies is immediate because the silica that the crystal is made of is also found in our bodies. What it reveals of life is in the form of new images and impressions that we've never had before. It's our responsibility to take what's best for us.

'You know a lot about the subject, don't you.' wondered Rémy.

'I could give you a lesson, all things being equal!', certified Anselme.

'I think I just got one!'

'Far from that! I'm so fascinated by it all that I could talk to you for days about! In addition, I am sure that the animals react too, but how? That was the question!'

'It's quite realistic Anselme, can you imagine if the dinosaurs had evolved in the same way as we have!'

Anselme laughed, and took on that direction.

'Yes, I can well imagine a world in which evolved prehistoric animals are carrying briefcases full of files, going to work, and schools with classes consisting of cute little T-Rex troublemakers in which a wise female dinosaur would teach them good manners!'

Rémy knowingly opened a parenthesis to relax Anselme, for he saw that that was a topic of conversation that was painful for him.

'Thanks Rémy,' said Anselme, moved looking at his friend in a friendly manner.

'But... for what my dear man, I did not do anything!'

'Rémy stop your charade!', he then looked him in the eye, smiling. 'For the first time in my life, I can talk about it without crying.'

'Well I'm listening!

'I really appreciate that side of you... You knew really know how to go about it.' Said Anselme now relaxed.

'So, go ahead; free yourself...'

'It's just... I don't knew where to start.'

'Try at the beginning...!

'I'm starting... I remember that day, it was fine, a beautiful day was coming. Every morning, I went to take Drakkar out for a walk. It was a Saturday and I had to repair a part of the fence in the garden that had been damaged by the dog over the years. So when I got home, I told Constance that I was taking the car to go buy the necessary things in order to finish it that day. I took the wheel, I drove five minutes, and out of the village, Ms Granier, an old lady of eighty-two back then, now deceased, crossed the road without worrying about traffic; she crossed right in front of my hood and the only reaction I had was to avoid her. So I turned to the right and hit the brakes and I crashed against the wall of her house. I was told later in the hospital that I stayed in a coma for four days. When I woke up, I did not even remember having an accident. It took me some time before recovering my memory. But there was something else that bothered me: above all, I couldn't feel my legs, no more sensitivity, nothing!

'I saw the nurses, and I recognized them one by one, all taking care of me. As time went on, the more I was recovering my senses, the more I was aware of my state. Two weeks later, I found my thoughts and something happened that I can't explain – at least, not at that moment. I heard a voice that reassured me and comforted me. It was a little later that I realized it was you and I then remembered the relationship we had. Somehow, you helped me, but the day I realized that I did not get up too soon, all collapsed like that. I knew even before Ghislaine had told me. Besides, I only had to see the expression on Constance's face trying to clumsily to hide it from me, trying to stop my understanding. I felt as if my life stopped here in that hospital, I was stopped dead as in the tracks of life; time stopped for me. I looked like a skeleton to top it all off, the slightest gesture demanded a superhuman effort. I was no longer part of the "active". I began to understand the extent of the mental disaster inflicted by situations such as that, what it can cause especially when I was discharged to begin rehabilitation. Whenever important people visited me I was constantly in that unbearable suffering and it was impossible for me to express it to them; I felt that it went their completely above the head, they could never understand how I felt. I felt separated from the world.

'For me, only you and the others were able to understand and perhaps even Constance by her love for me; even if our relationship have become increasingly difficult and slowly deteriorated over the years… I gradually became odious with her, starting with making her feel my pain, and that, in spite of myself. But I couldn't control myself; the pain was too strong at that time. I didn't think she could even be unhappy. Looking back, I realized that it wasn't easy for her either. She told me later that she was reached a point where she had to take almost a dictionary for synonyms to say 'everything will work out.' Our phone conversations at night, which we used to have just before to bed, occupied her thoughts from the afternoon until the time we spoke. When she managed to fall asleep, it was never before two or three in the morning; and I have not seen it all. That experience has really put into question everything in our lives; to the foundations of our marriage. What do you want; we have all kinds of ghosts just waiting to resurface!'

'It's a human reaction Anselme. Those who "optimize" before even knowing, realize that sooner or later of the upheaval that such an experience brings; then you do not have to feel guilty for that. In addition, you have caught up since...'

'It's true; I think I have negotiated my own "mea culpa"! Regardless, I slowly began to realize... I became the ones I was treating. I could see the looks in their eyes when I comforted them. Certainly, they appreciated it because I've always been honest with them, but I was standing... And their eyes cruelly forced me to understand; I happened sometimes to cry in a corner, I really couldn't bear it. So after four months of fog in my mind, I made a decision, the best that I made in my life!

'Now that I knew the least that I could do for them and especially for you, it was to fight so that I'd walk again. That day, I knew that I will. Everyone in my professional field and even my friends had given up on me. Since then, I had only one thing in mind...

'"You don't believe; well, open your eyes that you will use later to weep in joy, when I get up in front of you, holding my right hand towards you, to greet you!"

'I was proud of myself, disabled, but proud... And it was precisely what I wanted to convey to Victor and to the others. It

39

was in my eyes the best way to give them courage. It's a strange little feeling, but in the end I was almost happy to have had that accident. Finally, I discovered what my mission was in life. And all my colleagues who condemned were going to realize what human will and motivation can do.

'For them, it was impossible that I would walk again. In addition, they had almost convinced my family who slowly began to lose hope. It made me push myself further when I was standing with the parallel bars. At first, I practically moved millimetre by millimetre, and then centimetre by centimetre, until the first small steps that added up by the day. I trained with a Walkman and headphones that I had Constance buy for me. The music I listened to was to motivate myself to go on and on, morning, afternoon, it became an obsession. Often I was told that I did too much, underlying the idea that the outcome was already determined. But I paid them no mind. I had certain advantages, being part of the staff myself, and I used them! I had to show them that they wrong. I became the hero of my own story! And there's that Ghislaine, one day, a nurse and colleague came to me during a session. At that time, it had been a little over two years I was in rehab. I saw her approaching and I decided to take a break. At the time, I did not understand the expression on her face. She staring at my legs and arms in an unusual way, and with great amazement. It looked like she had just seen a ghost. I didn't realize that I had let go of the bars and I was standing in front of her without any support.

'When I realized it, I fell into her arms and I burst into tears. I thought, "Finally, I did it, now I will walk." Hard to describe what I felt that day. It was a mixture of pride, accomplishment, and liberation, while at the same time. I imagined I had already gone home in an armchair, then standing up in front of Constance.

'When I got myself together, I made her swear to keep quiet until I am ready enough to make the surprise. Luckily, I was alone that day in the rehabilitation room. So I asked Constance to bring me one of my son Grégory's AC/DC albums. You cannot imagine how that music was catchy, though I've never really been a fan. But in that specific case, I especially enjoyed the spite of that music; each situation has its music! That was really an unforgettable day. So you see, there was not only the music that came out in me, but without it, as sure as the sun burns, I could not have succeeded. That's how it was for me...'

Anselme suddenly seemed ecstatic...

'What going on?' innocently asked Rémy.

'I don't really know; I feel relieved... I find that I haven't really absorbed my accomplished efforts. It's true that I had a lot of trouble!'

'Well, know that you have the admiration of all!'

'I realize that, but they did not tell me. Just between us, they should have told me.'

'They weren't allowed to.'

'Why?'

'They thought you had done enough as a nurse, and they did not want you to spend all your time with them. You had a family to take care of. I think they wanted to thank you in their own way. So they discussed again and again, day after day, week after week, and they eventually agreed. They didn't tell anyone else so as to surprise everyone. Their motivation was foolproof.'

'If I had expected it... I was miles away from thinking that I had inspired that!'

'They wanted above all to get out of their situation which they were in, for them, their family, for me and for you.'

Rémy watched Anselme who was literally stunned.

'So what do you say?'

'It's wonderful Rémy. Although I won't remember when I wake, thank you for giving me such a show.'

'The pleasure's mine, Anselme; and speaking of entertainment, the surprises are just beginning...'

'Why?'

6

Progress?

'The fool holds his heart on his tongue.
The wise man keeps his tongue over his heart.'
Heraclitus

Rémy put his hand on Anselme's shoulder.
'Now you know. Come, let's go.'
'Where are you taking me this time?'
'It only depends on you. That was what I call the "bonus" and you're not obliged to accept.'
'You're not just going to let me hang like that, are you?'
'I know, but what I'm proposing now, is a journey to the future where you can actually see the frame of mind I told you about, one hundred and seventy years from now.'
'Why so far?'
'Because we'll be two thousand one hundred and sixty...'
'So after that?'
'That's the time when people realize they have gone too far with technology; what do you say?'
'Why not, you know very well that I never refuse such getaways; in addition, it may be instructive, and we finally have the answers to the questions we asked ourselves as...'

'Some, but not all!'

'What do you mean?'

'We'll lose our way often; reality is a wholly different... the thought that man is capable of whatever wisdom no matter what happens is wrong. Aside from his natural curiosity, there are too many elements that must be taken into account. We imagined a bunch of scenarios, but we are far from the truth. Above all, I must explain a few details; the work of a famous teacher called "Kevin Warwick" in the United States of America, started in the nineteen-nineties. The first results will emerge in the year two thousand twenty, spawning a new era of cyborgs. Until then, he applied his research on himself, his collaborators operating on him. His body was riddled with electronic implants known as 'nano machines.' They greatly improved his physical and mental abilities, similar to the 'Six Million Dollar Man'; do you remember that series?'

Anselme approved with a nod, while Rémy carried on.

'He was capable of both physical and mental feats; the results were simply astounding. Of course, what was to happen, happened. Initially, the doctors made use of the technology to heal handicapped people, as it was a real technological revolution. People who were stuck on a wheelchair regained the ability to walk, quadriplegics were able to speak again in addition to being able to stand; the blind were able to see, but little by little, over the years it became a real business until that fateful time when everyone could be grafted with implants without having to be disabled. Some wanted to improve their mental ability to calculate faster than a computer, others wanted to record computer data into their brains, even more wanted to become physically stronger so to say, and that's just the beginning.

'Unbelievable!' cried Anselme amazed that, like an elementary school student, as he listened attentively to the words of his found friend!

'There were no wire or batteries in those implants; thereby they did not scare the candidates. But the turn of the tide doesn't wait. Cerebrovascular accidents happened quickly. It had become insane; a real "human chaos." Many lost their minds.'

'Well that's something,' said Anselme horrified.

'Fortunately, there were two categories of men because of you.'

'Because of me?'

'Yes, in some time you write a book in which you will make from your experience and your vision of humanity. You explain that it's useless to use technology to improve our capabilities because we were already capable, drawing on the ninety percent of our unused brain potential. You will show that man has always had timely control everything, leaving this undercurrent of fear of life, and somewhere, a refusal to evolve. You also explain to that technology should make life easier for some grunt work in a pinch, but must never replace us. Similarly, you will develop what you knew about the chromosome 'X' and 'Z'. But despite that, you will not succeed in opening everyone's eyes. Hence the appearance of those cyborg people who swear by the electronic progress. It was certain that results were faster, but they were only implants, "additives", and did not come from man himself. It was a type of assistance. In other words, if a nano-robot stops working for one reason or another, it inevitably becomes the carrier will revert back to who they were before the procedure; while those who would have developed their potential remain masters of their own power; they depend on nothing other than their own brain. All the progress they have made will be acquired.'

'It's true that all that reflects my state of mind,' said Anselme completely amazed. 'But I'll need whole two days while dreaming to see all that!'

'You've only been dreaming for ten minutes.'

'Only?'

'So what's your decision?' asked Rémy, who became his "time-less guide" for the night.

'Let's go! But why would you show all that, if I'm not going to remember anything when I wake up?' he insisted again.

'If you don't like it, I can leave you to your original dream and go away!'

'Of course not; I'll follow you...!' *Jerk,* added Anselme in thought.

'I heard that!'

'Whatever; it's the truth!'

Rémy greatly enjoyed his outspokenness; or rather his 'frank thoughts' in that case. The journey lasted as long as a single passing from one room to another in a house.

'We're already there? Whose place is this?'

'We're at Mr. and Mrs. Dumont's. I chose this place because they perfectly represent those who trust you and I was just as surprised as you are going to be. Now shut up, listen and watch!'

'Yes Sir!'

Rémy looked amused. Both were standing in the living room of the house of the family of two children and their parents. It was 5:30 p.m. ...

'Hello Mom, you're already done with work today?'

'I asked to be sent home early to spend some time with you. How's your cancer today?'

At that moment, Anselme was frightened. He looked to Rémy, eyes full of questions. The 'guide' simply put his finger in the mouth, accompanied by a knowing look. "Shhh... listen!"

'The rashes are all gone and I my fever's almost, don't worry!'

'Have you taken your medicine?'

'No, I didn't take, but I'm not worried because I know it'd pass.'

'You really are your father's son!' replied the worried mom. 'Listen to me,' she continued looking at the child's eyes, 'although today that disease is no longer considered deadly, there are still two percent of people who still die of cancer today; so you'll let me fret over you when the doctor diagnoses you with cancer.'

'Yes mom, I love you too!

'Out of my sight now; and do your homework in your room!'

'Already there! That's dad landing; I'll tell him everything's alright and I'll head up!'

Anselme could not believe his eyes and ears.

'Am I hearing right?' he asked, turning toward Rémy?

'Yes, your ears aren't deceiving you. For them, it's been more than forty years that they have integrated gradually your thinking into their lifestyle. The previous generation talked about it, and it was implemented. Of course, the boy did not need music to heal, because as you said, just now, that music was only one possibility among others, but at the time where we are, it's now commonplace. It's rooted in their minds, know cancer's 'overheating process', just as they know that a wound heals or that an angina can be treated in approximately two weeks. Two percent of people with that disease who die, are people who harboured evil in their lives. It's like the placebo effect... The ninety-eight other get rid of cancer as they would the common cold!

'That's fabulous; is the same for other deadly diseases?'

'That was the case for a large number of them because they discovered that our minds carried a great responsibility.'

'You mean our quality of life, work, stress... etc...?'

'Yes, but not only that. I speak of the 'mental state'; it is the state of mind in which you were at the beginning of the twenty-first century and it has long been elsewhere. You should know that man develops between ten and one hundred cancers daily depending on the level of stress you have. All are systematically eliminated thanks to our natural immune systems, but whether a day or a period of time is more or less stressful, the system weakens. In addition, the cancer will be fixed in specific locations depending on the problem that pollutes your life. For example for women, the most common is breast cancer which usually stems from a problematic childhood. And I'm just talking about cancer here, but the principle was the same for all diseases. In my lifetime, I have never heard of cancer viruses, or Alzheimer's floating in the air. We develop it, or we don't and that's it! And the fact that they exploit their capabilities as they do represent a real revolution. With improvements in the quality of personal, familial, professional, lives among others, man renews his cells easily. All you need is a bit of physical and mental training. The evidence is right under your nose: if you don't train yourself, you get nothing. It was the same for neurons, if they're not in use not, they die. But it was up to man to maintain and regenerate them. Of course, that was only one factor among many others. Personal or family problems are just as important.'

'And it took a hundred and seventy years to get there!' wondered Anselme.

'Yes my friend; How many centuries will it take to live as you live in your era?'

Anselme agreed with a discreet nod.

'One step after the other, Anselme, thus how men operate! The little I've lived made me realize that for most of us, we basically live for "getting something" in life. I talk about an enterprise, for example, or the "great job" that pays a lot of money. All is dedicated to money. But, apart from a few exceptions, do you think that billionaires are really happy?

'Because once you have everything you want, what's left after that, if you don't know how to live for something beyond your assets? Many "moneybags" lose some values because they realize that with time that everyone has a price; we are only human beings...

'But that was only one reason among many others. It will be established later that we and we alone are the main triggering factor.'

'What do you mean?

'It's all psychological. We all have diseases in us; we have the power to trigger them, and of course, if they can be provoked, one can naturally stop them. It's like a machine that you get to work when you press "On" and vice versa by pressing "Off". It's that simple!

'But it will take time for that 'shape-thought' to anchor permanently in the mind. Man's aspirations evolve according to the consequences of his own mistakes...

'The main thing was that we become aware one day,' punctuated Anselme; Moreover, 'we see more and more cases where people miraculously overcome diseases and deadly situations, forcing them to draw strength from deep within themselves, without knowing of its existence, much less how they work.'

'It's called the survival instinct,' said Rémy. 'And it is by seeing these so-called "exceptional" cases that attitudes were somewhat changed. There will be one in seven years at the time in which you live.'

'So in two thousand and twenty; and what is it?'

'It'll be a hiker who left alone from his home in December twenty-nineteen. But an avalanche will bury him completely.

Gone for just a afternoon, he'll only return home in February two thousand and twenty!'

'How would he do it?'

'Unconsciously, his body has cooled slightly, his heart slowed to a beat per hour...'

'A bit like being in a coma?'

'Yes, but in that case, we're talking hibernation...'

'Wait a second... hibernation?'

'Yes Anselme, that's what I said!'

'So, they have already put into practice at that time?'

'No, not yet, it will happen much later. Can I continue without you interrupting me every two minutes?'

'Death didn't relieve you of your attitude! Carry on, I won't butt in any more.'

'It was therefore during snowmelt that he gradually regained his senses and eventually recovered, albeit weakened, but enough to be able to move. He returned home without knowing that it had been more than two months!'

'Damn, two months!' thought Anselme dumbfounded.

'I'll let you imagine the many reactions that that story aroused. His family thought he was dead, but also physicians themselves would hardly believe it; and yet they will be unable to prove otherwise. They will even doubt his word suspecting him of having spent the winter warm somewhere with an accomplice. But how to explain his empty stomach? It will be appreciated later in his library is a book written by the hand of a certain Anselme Leroy...

'The book I'll be writing?'

'Yes, exactly! You will be so explicit and convincing that a lot of people, just like that man, will tap into their dormant resources without even realizing it. It was at that time that humanity will begin to want to tap into those new capabilities that are in us, not in one fell swoop, but as they say, the machine will be running!'

'Won't you look at that, he said "us" as if he was still alive...' observed Anselme, despite himself. 'I totally agree with that,' he went on. 'I always thought that we know nothing of ourselves.'

'I heard...'

'What?'

'I heard your mind; just like your surprise at that story of two months in the cold.'

'Oh yes, it's true! Well, I...'

'Don't worry, it's nothing; you'll always feel like a man after your death, but you will have the feeling of being the best, that's all. Finally, almost everything...'

Anselme said nothing and remained 'pale' for moments.

'It's alright!' Rémy reassured him, seeing him embarrassed.

'No, I wasn't thinking about that; you just opened a door in me... At least I think so! You didn't see that one coming huh?'

'No, I admit it; I didn't even try. Well, let's close that parenthesis and carry on, if you do not mind.'

'Please Rémy, carry on.'

'You said that we do not know each other and you are quite right. The previous generations from the present time, have taken a beating, and gradually they reverted to the values of "old" while continuing to live with technology that has not stopped evolving. On the flip-side, they have also evolved in the right direction if you will, because evolution remains same and will continue its way against all odds; that's what we were doing that makes it good or bad. For example, that family we visited was much more advanced than you in two thousand and thirteen. They all have at least developed an ability or a capacity, if you prefer. The mother often communicates with the father by telepathy;

51

the boy developed his ability to see events that will occur in the near future and the daughter who's three years older has started to master telekinesis. Yet they only operate between fifteen and twenty percent of their potential. That's what studies say in that period. Furthermore, their Life expectancy is between a hundred and twenty and one hundred and forty! Which is not always the case with 'nano-robots.' And all that is worth as many points that will gradually tilt the trend. Do you now see what happens to those who have not taken you seriously?

'Now that I've seen that, sometimes twice a day!'

'And you will be served... ! At the time, neuroscientists such as Jeff Hawkins in the US or Alain Cardon in France were significantly ahead for a long time, and the first 'beings' with a form of robotic conscience named "Pleo", who had the appearance of a cute little dinosaur created by Mr. Caleb Chang is relegated to antiquity. All three worked in the two thousands. These researchers had finished by breaking through the mysteries of the neocortex which as you know, is two millimetres thick and consists of six successive and separate the layers located on the outside of the brain. To achieve their goal, they had to decipher and transcribe into computer codes all the mechanisms of human thought. Upon success of their project, the applications have been numerous. We could explore the unknown seabed or other planets by sending those beings with artificial intelligence, thus able to make decisions for themselves. But one day, everything went to hell. They shared with those machines a consciousness that was proprietary to man by right. Soon, those robots gained little by little feelings, desires, demands and rants; finally, they become uncontrollable as the man... in the the end, after almost a century of developments in the field, those who swore by electronics finally wanted to robotize themselves to better gain control. In any case, they thought...

'Are you ready?

'I will not let you go an inch!'

Just as quickly, they went to the other side of the city of the 'Martins' and came upon a family that did not plan to live without electronics and implants...

The father tinkered in the garden, building a hut for his young seven year old son who had no implant, because rues required that parents must leave the choice to their children; and apart from some unscrupulous doctors, they put no implants on a child under the age of sixteen – which became the legal age at that time. To Anselme's amazement, the father raised and carried loads of boards weighing more than two hundred pounds piece. Suddenly he stopped working and puts his hand on the head, as if to prevent something from coming out. At that point, he curled up pain, stayed on the ground and focuses, much like Rodin's 'The Thinker'. He just received a text message, as if a computer on two legs, explained Rémy. The message was displayed on the retina of his right eye, which underwent an operation, like a TV viewer in front of his screen. Furthermore, his 'Super-eye' had the ability to see clearly at a distance of three kilometres!

'Extraordinary!' punctuated Anselme, privileged witness of that unprecedented scene!

Meanwhile the mother, who had gone out to do some shopping, came walking with a speed of more than seventy kilometres per hour, thanks to implants in her legs. Approaching the house, she opened the door from a distance and puts a few devices to work.

Anselme was flabbergasted; he had the impression of observing the shoot of a science fiction film.

But she reacted badly to the operations and that day, she started to short-circuit for some time in the kitchen under the frightened eyes of her sister, who used a more conventional means of locomotion to visit her; she could only watch, powerless, that sad spectacle; she had never adapted to that form of progress.

'It's hard to believe,' said Anselme, watching in concern with Rémy. 'I find it hard to believe that our body can endure all that, although I knew that we can surprise ourselves sometimes. But most of all, how could we fall so low?'

'That's going to be within the reach of everyone, you know; ignorance is not an option during assembly, it's to be universal and everyone can enjoy it.'

'A bit like stupidity!'

'That's a very funny parallel…

'And Earth… I hardly dare ask you what will happen to the Earth with all those changes taking place!'

'You mean the continents, the climate…?'

'Yes exactly; we hear a lot about global warming right now, and I'd like to see how it all evolved.'

'With regards the continents, they have not moved much in this time, but I have indeed seen some radical changes in the landscape elsewhere. You want to go have a look?'

'Might as well!' said Anselme trying to hide his excitement; 'It'll be a change from these electronic plastic people!'

The two then began to take off and fly over the landscape towards the coast, like Superman in his morning air jog.

Maybe it can be called "the morning sky-ing". Anselme saw the mountains, cities, and rivers roll by at full speed as if he were on a plane.

'You sure I'll remember absolutely nothing?'

'Absolutely sure. You'll get the information, but at the sub conscious level, well-stored in one of the drawers of your soul.'

'In one of the drawers of my soul? I have rather thought about drawers in my brain...'

'The brain is only a support, an organ; do I need to teach you? It's our soul that stores a piece of information not a bit of meat, which takes the same way our body does when we breathe our last breath, every single time...'

'Of course; then I will work to turn it to dust of those days!' he joked.

'It's quite possible if you put your mind to it; but take care that old unpleasant memories do not recur at the same time.'

'I hadn't thought of that detail.'

'I know, and that's why I'm telling you.'

'But if we were capable of so much, we can also control that phenomenon...'

'You can be quite the mutton-head Anselme! Whether you like it or not, you're like all the people around you, even if you have a mind that's a little more open. You're not trained for that. It's like all things that deserve special attention. If you do not have the habit of practicing, you can easily go astray and you won't know where you are.'

'At least when you were alive, you didn't have the answer for everything!'

'That's normal, I was one of the mortals. But for what little you show of your credentials when you die, some privileges are granted.'

'What does that mean? How? By whom?'

'Calm down! It means that we always get what we deserve; we prepare our deaths ourselves, just like retirement which is why we make contributions... But that's a bit more singular, because it's that of life. Shortly before my death, I was already having fun walking around as I am doing with you. But I had a choice I cannot speak of to you today and now that I think of it, I have made that choice a long time ago.'

'Can I have something less vague, or will I have to content myself with that?'

'Be grateful and look down. It might not be much at first glance, but if you look closely, there's change.'

'In what part of the world are we?'

'We flew towards the southeast. We're now above where once stood the French Riviera.'

'What! But where is it?'

'It practically doesn't exist anymore! Only a few atolls remain. The water rose thirty to forty meters and engulfed most of the cities and villages that were located along the shores and beaches.'

'You knew it all didn't you?'

'I had plenty of time! But that will be our last break, because I have shown you too much already.'

'Why? On the contrary,' Anselme was like a child discovering world; besides, I won't remember so…'

'Yes, but it's got nothing to do with your earthly life; in other words, with the best of intentions, you will never live it.'

'I think I understand what you mean. But before leaving again, I have one last favour; let me look at it again for a moment, it's really impressive. Thinking I have trodden the streets of some of those cities and I haven't seen more than a few roofs of buildings, sent shivers down my back. What happened to the people who lived there?'

'From what I could see, they were saved except some who wanted to remain against all odds. The rise of the waters spread over nearly fifty years. So they had time to see it coming. It was not like a devastating tsunami.'

'And that long gray line that's popping up in some places, I assume that's the highway that joins Spain to Italy, right?'

'Yes, it certainly looks like it.'

'We could still drive over on that section we see here.'

'Yes, but if you were coming over there, for example,' continued Rémy, pointing to a lake where a few peaks of buildings emerged, 'you would find yourself under water! That said, they could not fix it somehow... there, look there's one coming...'

'What?

'Look... slightly to your left, to the sky...'

'I'd just like to confirm; is this within the scope of my life on Earth?'

Rémy seemed to have trouble answering.

'Yes and no... you'll probably know the start of it. Look or you might miss it.'

Anselme saw something fly at a distance. It approached, barely making any noise; certainly not as fast as an aircraft or as big, but he could not define what it was.

When the machine was about a hundred yards away, he began to make out the shape of the flying object.

"But what was that thing?" He thought. "No, that's not true... it looks like..."

Rémy looked at him with a smile...

'But it's... it's a car!' exclaimed Anselme.

'Not quite,' said Rémy; 'it's an "aerocar"!'

'A what?

'An A-E-RO-CAR!'

'They could give it a name other than that one!'

'They went with the most logical, an automobile travels on land and an aerocar in the air!

'"Lapalisse" wouldn't have fared better. But, they still have wheels?'

'Nothing escapes you Anselme. As far as I know, having

observed closely for long moments, those are cars and aerocars in one. The wheels were kept so as they could be driven, because at first, not all who wanted to fly flew, it was regulated... they weren't allowed to fly over three hundred meters and there was a new license to pass. The other factor was geographical... Only people who were close to flooded areas were eligible to buy one; but they have had to control them less and less, because I always see more when I come in this half century. It must be recognized that they were very simple and practical; I have seen several parked in car parks, and I must say it was quite surprising; there was no need for space to manoeuvre, people get into their aerocars, close the door and take off vertically, then horizontally! All with the smoothness to make the earlier UFO designers cry with jealousy!'

'But, why did they create those items? They could just as easily use boats to go to flooded places and good old cars on the remaining roads – there's still much left anyway.'

'Since two thousand and thirty, there was no more oil and car manufacturers had to focus on that new mode of transport and travel. So they started developing electric cars worldwide. They first developed models with self-rechargeable batteries via photovoltaic solar panels placed on their roofs and had a system amplifying the effect of sunlight. At first only the wealthy could afford them but manufacturers have made a great gamble in producing millions of units and they therefore became cheaper. Later, not everyone wanted to move from the completely or partially submerged areas, and knowing that the rise of water had reached its limit, they created the first aerocars that had the same success as cars did.'

'How do they fly?

'There are two stabilizing fins you saw below, which are

deployed, and they have six mini thrusters equipped with an electrical operating system. There's one at each corner the vehicle and two at the rear; moreover, it was possible to control the power they develop with an embedded controller. The system took almost a century to perfect. In the first years, they were mostly seen around flooded like London, Shanghai, Bangkok or New York, to name only foreign cities. Then it spread to our place where French manufacturers, German, Spanish and Italian, took on the competition.'

'Wait a minute... Why do you say that the water level has reached its peak, so there will no longer be glaciers at that point?'

'There's still a bit, but they're too soft... Permafrost, or if you prefer methane (greenhouse gasses) that was trapped in the large expanses of ice for millions of years, was released as they melted, thus accelerating the warming.'

'That's a vicious cycle!'

'Absolutely,' Rémy nodded. 'The North Pole has become a vast extent of land surrounded entirely by water, and the Himalayas which still has the highest peaks in the world, no longer has snow and thus no longer has its large ice caps in the past. But the most disastrous is the Amazon...'

'There was never any ice there,' wondered Anselme.

'No, but today it's a barren desert, as it was the most humid place on the planet...'

'How could such an area lose its moisture?'

'The trees; the vegetation no longer did its work in absorbing oxygen. And since we're on the subject, in seven billion years, the Earth will no longer exist because it has been cooked by the sun which would've grown sixteen times larger, and two hundred times hotter.'

'We travel more towards death than life!' joked Anselme. 'You've gone up to that time?'

'No,' said Rémy with a smile, 'I saw it in a documentary on TV with the people we just visited!'

'You are such prankster,' said Anselme, a bit thoughtful.

'What's going on?'

'So, that's what awaits us!'

'Not you, but your children and grandchildren will live through it… Come, we must go now.'

'One more detail please… if you could do as much things when you were alive, why didn't you use it?'

'We'll talk… about it again.'

He paused, then continued.

'How many were you at my funeral?'

'I must admit that we were not numerous.

'You were four!'

'I'm sorry Rémy, I shouldn't have asked that question.'

'Don't worry about it… Let's go back now; you'll have to wake up shortly.'

'Will I see you again?'

'Soon enough, my friend.'

Anselme wanted to give him a friendly hug to show him everything what he felt at that time, but all he held was air.

'I don't understand, how could you take me by the hand earlier?'

'It wasn't you in the flesh who was with me, but your energy, or your mind if you understand it better. At the beginning you were able to because we were in your dream, but we managed well enough, but from here on in, you'll need practice.'

'Meaning…?'

'Let's say it was my dream at the end; you were in my territory!'

'Like…'

'Shush! Be quiet!'

Anselme stared Rémy,
'So it's "see you soon", right?'
'Yes Anselme… See you soon.'
The atmosphere was intense, almost palpable, as the friendship in their eyes was great. The moments he dreamed seemed so real to him. He wanted so much to keep them memories, but 'such was death' Rémy would surely say. Anselme suddenly saw Rémy move away, waving at him.
'Goodbye,' he whispered.
Anselme had already begun REM sleep and slowly left his dream.

7

Such is an expedition...

'The great art of being happy is the art of living well.'
Jean-Louis Guez de Balzac

Meanwhile in Grégory's car, Sofia and Constance spent time discussing everything and nothing all at once, a few times punctuated by Greg's interventions.

'How was it that we have received your invitations?' questioned Sofia.

'If I understand the little note that came with it, it's from people who knew Anselme well. He took care of them, a few years back. Today, they want to give him his proper due, all the while being discreet about it. I didn't question it because I knew the person who wrote the message.'

'That was quite unusual, don't you think?'

'Yes, but it did not surprise me. After his accident, he found himself in the same situation and has invested heavily in music.'

'Was it a shock to you?'

'Ho, yes! He who loves to ride, walk, swim in the lake ten kilometres from Saint-Just, found himself suddenly stuck in a wheelchair for almost three years, in the company of those he treated. I can tell you that the shock that I felt from was not his!

Three to four months went by before he got his act together and decided to move on.'

'Between three and four months! Many people who manage to such an accident, often take years to recover from the shock and regain a taste for life.'

'You're right,' confirmed Constance; but since I live with him, many things that seemed obvious before, are no longer so today. For a man like him, three to four months to be depressed is a lot! However, if we look a little closer, I admit he quickly recovered.'

'But was he really disabled?'

'What do you mean by that?'

'Forgive me, that was clumsily worded. I just wanted to say that few people manage to get back up.'

'Yes, I am aware and I know I was very lucky to have met him.'

'I don't doubt it. I would even say that if it had not happened, I never would have met Greg; isn't that right, my love?' she concludes putting her hand on his face.

'Okay dear, what do you want?' Greg joked.

Knowing his son, Constance knew the joke well, but chided him gently,

'Ho my boy! Well, I did not raise you like that!'

'Well, never mind, I still stand by what I said!'

Constance noticed the change in her son from his turbulent past. That day, she saw a responsible father, lover and proud of his child. That new personality was more balanced, relaxed, and successfully forgot the clashes of the past.

The two women launched an amused look and continued their discussion with gusto.

'Like I said before, Anselme was someone who believes in his fate and especially himself. He is from a generation where we constantly talk about 'God', but he has more confidence in his own abilities, than that of the great sage white beard as he says!'

Sofia had a moment of surprise. Hearing Constance talk allowed her to consider a stepmother with 'easy access', with whom she can be comfortable with in constructive discussions.

'Yes, excuse me Sofia, I let myself go a little!'

'Don't be offended for me. Unlike my parents, I am not at all connected to any religion.'

'That was what I found listening to them talk. Since we are on the tpic, they must join us after tomorrow, isn't that right?'

'Yes; they will soon be with us, but my father started working on the roof of their house that he could not leave unfinished. In addition, they already have a pool in the garden!'

Sofia presented with such seriousness, thus letting her 'tongue-in-cheek' side show, so as not to displease her company.

It was a little more than two hours and a have that they have been on the road. Constance suggested a stop to stretch their legs. Sofia used her mobile phone to tell Véronique.

Véronique's ringtone was set to maximum volume, perfectly imitating the takeoff of a Boeing 707. It immediately woke Anselme and the two children upon the first ring.

"Shit, the buzzer!," She thought.

Confused, she apologized and prepared some change to buy hot drinks and possibly snacks. Both cars soon stopped on a motorway service. Once in the parkinglot, everyone went down and began by stretching. As it was not quite eleven, Sébastien, proposed to take a short break to make the second one longer, when they would stop for lunch. Everyone agreed. They walked to the entrance and went straight to the toilet by setting go to the bar located in the large service station boutique. Their tasks done, they held a meeting, sitting around one of the tables provided.

'Children, sit quietly!' Said Sofia like a school mistress.

'He didn't snore too much, did he?' asked Constance to Sébastien, nodding towards Anselme.

'Not the slightest bit!' He assured her. 'But I've never seen Dad smile so much in his sleep!'

'Between you and me, me neither, he was probably dreaming of something funny!'

Constance remained thoughtful for a moment. She suddenly remembered one night when she watched her beloved smiling in his sleep... and discussing aloud with someone known.

'I don't even remember,' said Anselme.

Suddenly, the voice of a lady rang in the shop.

'Rémy!'

Anselme turned abruptly toward the voice.

'Don't go too far,' said the lady was talking to a young child! A little puzzled, he returned to his coffee cup.

'Are you okay, dear?' asked Constance, alarmed.

'Yes darling, I'm okay; I'm only trying to wake up...'

'How much longer are we driving?' asked Véronique to her husband.

'Between five and six hours.'

'We better not wait too long,' continued Sébastien.

'You're right,' said Constance. 'Let's finish our drinks and let's go. We can't be late.'

'Late for what?' innocently asked Anselme.

'You don't don't miss a chance, do you!'

'He tried once earlier when we left!' emphasized Véronique.

'You dared!'

'Alright! Come on, kids, finish your drinks and let's go.' concluded Anselme, teasingly.

Five minutes later, everyone went back into the cars and continued their trip. The children went back to sleep quickly.

Tired, Constance leaned in turn. Without knowing why, Anselme tried to do the same, but in vain.

'Can't go back to sleep, dad?' asked Sébastien.

'No, but don't worry about me; just keep your eyes on the road,' he retorted. Anselme seemed preoccupied.

Sébastien noticed, and preferred to keep his silence.

'And you my angel, aren't you getting some sleep? You didn't sleep a wink since we got up that morning. You have two good hours before you!

'I hear you, my dear. See you later.'

'Sleep well; I'll wake you when we arrive.'

Taking her turn, she made herself comfortable, and slept like a log.

Anselme said nothing and watched the landscape roll by. Upon approaching a highway exit, he saw in the distance a billboard advertisement. He did not make out the content, but he could not help the look. Gradually, as they approached, he could see two huge eyes within which a brand of glasses were written. The eyes were taking up all the space. In that moment, it was as if all his past suddenly came back to him seeing that image. It was Rémy... They were his eyes. It was the whole story... But the 'signs' did not stop there. A little later, he figured what appeared to be a nightclub. There, he saw a black silhouette on a bright background light. He tried to mind it, but he couldn't help it, he couldn't tear his eyes away. What could it all mean? Was it the figment of his imagination or an unusual conspiracy? Questions raced through his mind and he began seriously to consider the unthinkable.

Much later, the two cars cut a convoy of five minibuses apparently accompanied by other cars that appeared to be part of the convoy. Again, a detail struck him. Aboard many of those vehicles were wheelchairs, folded neatly in the back. All that became more and more disturbing and Sébastien noticed the face of his father fall over the distance.

'You alright, dad?' he asked him, a little worried.

'I don't know; I think I'm being haunted by ghosts.'

'We can talk about it if you like.'

'I'll tell you one day, but not today. I prefer to stay in my thoughts for now. No offense, alright?'

'No, don't worry, it'll have to take more than that.'

'But don't worry too much, it's nothing serious. Drive well, and drive us safely, son.'

'No problems, dad.'

Meanwhile, in the other car, Grégory began to show signs of fatigue.

'Don't you want to stop you and let me drive?' asked Sofia.

'If it becomes necessary, you'll drive; but for now I'm alright.'

Sofia knew that even when tired, he enjoyed driving. She didn't insist, but did take on the job to keep talking to him, to help fight off drowsiness. However, she was reassured by the fact was responsible enough to give her the wheel if it became too hard for him to continue.

8

Review

'The best mirror does not reflect the other side of things.'
Anaïs Nin

Meal time had already gone for more than an hour. The dashboard clock showed one-fourty in the afternoon, while another motorway service would be reached in two more kilometres. On the signpost, listed among other services, was the word 'RESTAURANT'. That time, no one took the trouble to ask any further; both cars went straight there. Everyone headed for the place and sat around a table. Anselme said nothing; he always seemed preoccupied. Constance noticed but did not try to pry; she decided to simply watch him from the corner of her eye. Everyone spoke of different topics just like each time they had the opportunity to do so at a family meal. But Anselme was still absent. Not wishing to be a spoilsport, he listened to snippets of conversations to try to mix it up, but did not have the mind to 'communicate'. He suddenly heard the conversation between Grégory and Sofia...

'With this promotion our troubles will be over, darling. Furthermore, we'll be near the sea, on the French Riviera; it will be great for Gérémi...'

Anselme could not hold himself back and had a strong reaction. He rose halfway, both hands on the table and shouted.

'Don't you ever do that!'

The way he had to say that, froze any attempt at a response.

'Hey, Dad, what's wrong with you?'

Anselme reacted very rarely so and did not know what to reply. Confused, he put his hand over her mouth as if to prevent other words from getting out.

'I'm sorry. I don't know what came over me.'

He sat back and shut himself up in his silence.

The only time Constance had seen him so anxious was back at the time of his disability. She wanted to know more, but chose to give up and postpone. Everyone around the table was rather shocked at the unexpected brutish reaction. They did not know what to say to relax the atmosphere. Anselme noticed and prepared to reassure them when suddenly a gravelly, shrill, yet feminine voice, was heard in the whole restaurant.

'I pinch your nose, and milk, it flows!'

It was a 'roadster-woman' who was talking to a young driver; she lived in Saint-Just with her husband. Only blind and deaf people had not notice her presence in the village. Like a lioness protecting her cubs, Anselme took the word.

'Don't you ever look back and continue to eat as if nothing happened!'

Constance could not help but giggle. Grégory and Sébastien had heard about it; Sofia and Véronique sought to understand, and the children did not have much to do.

'Tell them,' said Constance.

'You really think it's worth it?' he replied, amused.

'It'll give us a good time, don't you think!'

'Yes, you're right... You knew Yannick's son, Bernard?'

Grégory and Sébastien both answered in the affirmative.

'No, not you, you have grown up together! Well, for you girls, I speak of the son of our neighbour who was a truck driver; on weekends, he parks his truck on the large car park, just down Saint-Just. You might've noticed it when we left?'

Sofia nodded, turning to Véronique who did the same.

'Next to his truck are parked two more owned by Ines and Rocco, a couple of truck drivers arrived in the village three years ago. One Sunday, when we invited them along for drinks at home, Yannick told us a story so funny, you'd bust your gut laughing! You should know that he was not one to get angry easily and yet believe me, some jokes truly are lost on him! It's been two months they had reached Saint-Just. On the parking lot, she had already taken the privilege of wanting, demanding and, incidentally, gave you hell if you did not do what she asked, while Yannick, parked in it for more than seven years. You noticed the little bushy hedge that separates the parking lot from the main road, right?'

All nodded and looked forward to more.

'Parking along those bushes, was a guarantee of security for any night visits. I speak of diesel theft to name an example. Yannick often left them in those places, but one day, he did not want to calculate anything; he parked directly along the bushes, thus along the road. And now the next day she cornered him and pointed out to him kindly in him saying, "You took my place!"

'Of course, he did not expect that at all. But that's not all! Meeting her squarely, he asked her why she wanted to park only at that place and not in any another. She told him, as naturally as you please, that she found the bushes very cute! He understood very well that at that point, the truck was at the sight of all, so it was less likely to be visited. He saw that she did not want to share.

'But he wasn't completely stupid. When she realised that the pretty bushes were not fully appreciated, she called on a lot of reasons, one more preposterous than the one before. He even ended up wondering if there was the word "fool" etched on his forehead!

'Yannick did not believe her capable of invoking a "golden" excuse like that for a simple parking space; moreover, he fell from so high, he remained silent! After, there were many others, but since then his nickname was easily found!'

At that time, hilarious, Anselme resumed,

'Children, let me introduce you to "Pretty Bush"!'

Everyone snickered quietly, but the heart was there. Puzzled by what she heard, Sofia wanted to know more...

'How old is she? I have some trouble picturing her; she must surely be young and arrogant.'

'It's true that these days, fifty years old or more is considered young!'

'More than fifty years old! And her husband said nothing, was she surprised?'

'People who live near a volcano do not seek to tame it, they live with...'

'Beautiful analogy,' said Sofia, 'but couldn't he pour some water on the fire?'

'I return your compliment! He probably could, but I doubt he would spend his life playing fire-fighter over marital fires, thus a peaceful life; what do you want, perfectionism would not exist if we were all perfect! Otherwise, Yannick readily admits he has not had good reactions on his side. He explained that at that time, he was uneasy; and it's true that I knew him to be much more reactive in those kinds of cases. But life forces us to challenge ourselves constantly, once you really try to understand the trials, which are always presented to us on time. And Yannick was of that caliber. He later confided jokingly to me that he probably preferred the gravel near those bushes since they were smoother, much less damaging for his truck's tires; or the shade of the big tree under which they park...'

'And then,' resumed Véronique, 'what did he do?'

'The roof of his trailer was a long plastic sheeting, which can optionally soften under the effect of a large continuous heat, and it dragged out on the road...

'Really?

Anselme smiled.

'Of course not, but it was well worth a natural history of bushes, do not you think?'

Amused, Constance said, 'Acknowledge that without it, you would not have relaxed sooner!'

'We must tell Yannick that for once, his presence has been beneficial!'

The meal ended in a good atmosphere and lasted a little over an hour and a half.

It was 3:30 p.m. when everyone headed back to the cars. They still had a little less than three hours to go.

9

Nose-press

'Life is full of illusions. Among those illusions,
some succeed. They are the ones that become reality.'
Jacques Audiberti

H alf an hour had gone by since they left the restaurant.
After having a meal of a nice big steak with greasy
fries, Anselme felt bloated and fell asleep again. He
soon returned in dreams both fantastic and surreal. That time,
he did not need anyone to return to 'Méribell.' Thus, he was able
to see himself in the days when he worked there. He was fifty-two
years old, and everyone was there.

But the atmosphere was different. All in the clinic gave the
impression of fearing someone. Piercing through the usual
silence of the place, voices were coming from all sides and echoed
in the vast building...

'Attention please, straighten up, he's coming!'

But what was going on?

He decided to turn to walk the corridors to understand what
could scare them so much. Sylvestre, who usually had his tongue
wagging, made himself very small. The doctor of the clinic
never recoiled from anyone but he now seemed reserved. In

addition, it was freezing cold in the facility. Anselme continued his exploration; as he arrived at the start of a long corridor, at the end of which was a figure in white with long red hair. He hesitated to advance. That strange figure was shaped like a man as he approached, but his face seemed to have been held in a vice for several days. Gradually, as he came closer, his steps slowed and became hesitant. Who could it be? A nurse? Impossible! From its appearance, even from a distance, he or she would have frightened the sick. He decided to stop there and talk to them.

'Hello! Who are you…? Are you looking for something?'

The shape continued to slowly approach him without saying anything.

'Do you hear me? What are you looking for?'

The low light prevented him from accurately distinguishing what he saw. He slowly began to turn back, while 'They' continue to rise. When they came within ten meters of him, it stopped and said in a voice similar to that of ET the alien pulling his snake tongue.

' "SSSSS… Who were you?" '

Anselme had a frightened reaction, took three steps back, and answered.

'I work here, I'm a nurse. And yourself?'

Suddenly, the thing ran at him, both arms forward like a sprinter trying to beat his own record; at that time, he realized that what was coming at him at full speed was no more nor less than a woman with a T-Rex's mouth and all teeth. Long red hair down her waist, and a tail moved behind her. A snake tongue rhythmically went in and out of her big mouth; in its course, the animal kept saying something very odd in that circumstance that was just as…

' "SSSSS… Stay where you are, I'll squeeze your nose!" '

Anselme did not understand at all. Distraught, wasted no time and ran to escape the monster.

"But, what was it?"

He tried to open room doors and take refuge. The fifth one was good. He entered, closed the door behind him and took the time to breathe for a minute, while the 'Woman-Rex' continued to run giving the impression of having a grafted weights of five hundred pounds on each foot, shouting, ' "SSSSS… Stop, I'll squeeze your nose!" '

Suddenly, he regained his breath, he heard a man's voice.

'Anselme!' He turned abruptly. What, who was there?

'Rémy!?'

'But what are you doing here?'

'I had an accident, I cannot move and you cared for me! You look like you're

in a hurry, what happened to you?'

'Hurried…? That's the right word. That's pretty much me, yeah!'

'Hey; you when you dream, you don't use the back of the spoon to scoop up imagination!'

'What do you mean?

'Don' you think you pushed too far by making her have the jaws of T-Rex?'

'Yes; hey good imagination or not, that thing was on my heels and wanted to press my nose!'

'So, it's no big deal.'

'Come on; just take a look and you'll understand!'

'For that, it would have entered that room and I just heard it pass by, so you're safe.'

'That's right, I heard it too; but it could very well make a u-turn and come in here.'

'If she had seen you enter that room, don't you think that it would have come directly?'

'You're probably right...'

'Don't worry anymore, you're safe here.'

Meanwhile, the friendly monster with long teeth carried on, continuing to chase everyone it saw... ' "SSSSSS... I'll squeeze your nose! I'll squeeze your nose!" '

Like a military meeting in a besieged base, everyone regrouped in the garden in front of the building to find a solution to the 'T-Rex, nose pincher' problem.

Thus, Victor was in his wheelchair, called for the assembly to settle it once and for all. Dr. Tibert, head of the clinic, was present and sought to reassure them.

'She only wants your milk, that's why she constantly seeks to press your nose. It's really not that bad!'

Without really knowing how, Anselme and Rémy were there as well. Anselme was wearing a white coat and Rémy was in his bed. That did not prevent him from communicating with others to vote except for Anselme, because everything was like in his memory except for the T-Rex, which was the fruit of his fantasmagorical imagination caused by the conversation he had with his family about 'Pretty-Bush'.

Damien who always had a joke, exclaimed:

'Let's take our time, no use in being "congested" because she shouldn't be screwed with, and we'll be out cold once "Ebenoser Screwge" gets us!'

Anselme offered to send his dog Drakkar, but Sylvestre pointed out that he might get his muzzle pinched for his milk. Jean suggested a trap with a net. Odilon, a former policeman, expressed the idea to simply gun then down. Jérôme thought of filling a vat of milk to drown it.

Meanwhile, in the corridors, you could hear the thing shouting. "Come back, I want to squeeze your nose!"

'So,' Bertrand continued, 'we must decide now!

'Calm down,' said Dr. Tibert. 'There are worse problems.'

'Oh yes,' said Florent. 'I'd like to see you with a T-Rex in a white coat running after you to pinch your nose!'

'Harmless or not, we're sick of it!' said Hughes.

Suddenly, the thing threw the two big doors open, and screamed with its big mouth, ' "SSSSSS... I'll squeeze your nose!" '

Everyone panicked and ran away, protecting their noses, when suddenly a dark night brutally set in...

'Dad... Dad! Wake up, we're here.'

Anselme woke with a start.

'No, not the nose!'

'Dad, you were dreaming, weren't you?'

Anselme took a few moments to regain his bearings.

'Yes, and what a dream!' he said, gently recovering.

'Why did you put your hand on your nose! Is something smelly?'

'That, too, I'll explain it later,' he replied smiling...

10

I'm watching over you...

'Reality neither comes nor goes, because it never stays the same.'
Lao-Tzu

'What time is it?' asked Anselme.
'Seven-thirty, dad.'
'This is where you're booked?'
'You can say that.'
Anselme was somewhat amazed at the response from his son, but didn't get back up. The most immediately important was to put their things in the rooms, to take a breather then go eat in the hotel's restaurant, then have a good night's sleep.

Located near the 'Disneyland' park, the setting was lovely. Their respective windows overlooked a huge green, quiet and flowery meadow as would a prairie city. In its centre, a beautiful Japanese garden was cut by a small artificial river, over which were built two wonderful little wooden bridges in the same style. The whole was strewn with bonsai, plants and other Asian flowers. The family occupied three adjacent rooms. Sébastien, Véronique, Kevin and Angel in the first one, Grégory, Sofia and Gérémi in the second, and Anselme and Constance in the third. It was at eleven o'clock when everyone bid each other good night in front of their respective rooms. All were very tired from the journey and fell quickly asleep – save for Anselme, who was in top shape. He decided not to go to bed immediately and told Constance, who was beginning to fall asleep, that he will be going out for a walk in the large park. The outside temperature was nice for a winter evening; he opted for a simple sweater, left the reception and walked straight in front of him in the direction of 'mini-Japan', a three minutes' walk from the hotel. Not far from two small bridges were some benches arranged in way that a large part of the landscape could be appreciated; he went towards them and sat on one of them. It was serene, quiet and discreetly lighted. Anselme felt perfect harmony within that little piece of paradise. While he lay down at full length on the bench, he heard the noise of leaves behind him. Far from being worried, he turned incuriosity, saw nothing special, and immediately went back into his meditation. Two minutes went by until the noise came to distract him again. He turned again, persuading himself that it had to be the wind. He watched the tip of trees and other foliage around; no wind, nothing, it was dead calm. Did that cursed wind possess a prankster's spirit! At the time, a little anxious, he decided to take his initial position, he saw the foliage move a third time. In that moment, he did not take his eyes off of it. He thought that one of his two sons, Grégory and Sébastien would have been quite capable of such a prank. But at their ages! Trying hard to have logic take over, he tried to find an explanation. What could possibly happen with that whimsical foliage, of all those who were standing there, was the only one move.

'Is anyone there?' he asked, cautiously.

Sébastien... Grégory...

No answer came to him. He could not tear his eyes off the

bush, but still decided to return to his initial position after a few moments, thinking: if the 'midnight killer' rode behind me looking for a new victim, then so be it! But in any case, nobody took away that special moment he had decided to grant that bench. Moreover, he had his soul in peace. If there had been a danger, he would probably felt it and he would not have reacted so. Thus, he appreciated the true value of the half-hour that followed not paying the bush any mind.

He began to think about the trip in which they were all invited.

What was the purpose? Why all the mystery? Did they think for him to meet with the 'Dalai Lama'?

Not probably, he who talks of the patron of Christians as the 'Great Sage with the White Beard!' He thought that had replied Sébastien about the booking. Why had he said 'We can say that...' when he was asked if they had booked that place... He had a sudden realisation. There was someone else, someone who has carefully concealed their identity. But who! Not finding answers to that question, he stood up, turned back to the bush, 'Goodbye troublemaker' and he quietly went back to the hotel. As he said goodbye, the bush shuddered one last time...

'I think I said "Goodbye" already,' said Anselme sure of himself, and never turning back!

Once in the room, he put on his pyjamas, lay down and closed his eyes. When he began to fall asleep, a muffled noise came from under the sheets. He looked up at the ceiling and sighed and said to his sweetheart who had just welcomed him with an odorous gift, 'Good night to you too sweetie!'

That had the effect of exasperating him most. Not that it never happens; it happens to everybody, but it was right when he too was making an effort for it not to happen. Worse yet; he had the exclusivity of that treatment.

The next morning, the alarm went off will all sorts of bells at half past seven, Constance woke first and placed a kiss on his forehead. So he had a little trouble getting to sleep following the delicate aroma of 'cir-Constance', he turned his head toward that of his beloved, cracked her a smile by looking her in the eye and farted in turn with such power that the noise was heard throughout the floor! For once, she was upset and sulked as she headed towards the bathroom. Anselme, lay still for another fifteen minutes, displaying an air of satisfaction as if he had just won the national lottery. As he had not gone to the bathroom yet, the smell that filled the room was noxious, and thus Constance did not take more than five minutes to prepare and head down for breakfast. Everyone had to get there by eight-thirty. The atmosphere was somewhat tense. Véronique tried to hurry her steps as the children, of course, were already dying to go to the 'Disneyland' park. As their accommodations were not very far, they decided to take a public transportation that led them on site in less than five minutes. Everyone noticed the tension between Constance and Anselme. From pride, something that he had felt ever since he punched the bed, Anselme now felt embarrassed to have reacted so. In those cases, calling it 'awkward' was the least that can be said. Assuming that she knew the feelings he felt for her, he preferred to let a little water flow under the bridge before saying anything to push things to a boil and solve the problem, thinking that she would eventually speak. On her part, Constance thought he was exaggerating and reproached him by not making the systematic first step to open the dialogue. Thus, it could take a few times a day or two before the situation unlocked itself. Sébastien, who heard like everyone else at the hotel what happened at about eight o'clock, tried a neutral maneuver to relax the atmosphere. Knowing that they had met at an Italian restaurant, he had a hidden agenda and approached his mother.

'Today we're going to make everyone happy! The little ones will have fun in the park and we planned to eat Italian at noon. It seems that their carbonara's even better than the one made by its creator!

She smiled, but still showed her annoyance.

'Don't worry, this won'; last! Thank you my son.'

'Is it because of the fifteen-magnitude earthquake this morning?' asked Sébastien in jest.

Anselme heard the remark and tried in vain to hold back laughter, he tried to hide it by coughing. Constance was frankly amused over the ridiculous situation, but she didn't want to show it. For Sébastien, it was a fiasco. When the bus came close to the park entrance, the children became overexcited, the grandparents made faces as long as Nile, and 'Rest of the band' said not one word, but in reality were amused to see that the old couple supposed to have acquired the age of wisdom, to ignore each other as would newlyweds after their first fight. Indeed, the atmosphere was certainly tense, but not heavy. Apart from children who paid no more attention to the 'thirty-nine forty' war, the adults meanwhile, were secretly in stitches!

11

Providence

*'Such is the human mind, even while travelling:
at every moment, it occupies all the space it has.'
Jean Paulhan*

They arrived at the entrance, and opted to take the 'day pass'. Thus, they could go to all the attractions as much as they wanted. Everything was at will, outside catering. At 9:20 a.m., Anselme wanted another coffee. Upon hearing that, the children pouted; they had only one objective: to go on the rides. Also, the three women proposed to accompany the children to the sights, while the men could drink their coffee, setting appointments at the 'Space Mountain 2' about half an hour later. After trying in vain to reason with their father, the three men joined the attraction where their wives and children boarded, who had waited all that time to be able to ride, the place being so crowded. They made a sign off and decided to join in the queue. They were lucky to have only had fifteen people before them and waited no longer to ride the infernal roller-coaster. When it stopped, they saw among the people who came down, small delighted families with their leaping children. Sofia and Véronique came to kiss their husbands; Kevin, Angel and

Gérémi were still eager to continue their tour of the carnival, and Constance gave Anselme a look like a soldier watching his enemy in the white of eyes eyes, armed with a water pistol. Anselme and his two sons rode in turn. Concerned about that situation, which was becoming increasingly absurd, he presented apologies for the vacant seat he stepped over, located right next to where he settled. It was extremely rare in that often crowded ride, which was in the form of small trucks equipped with four seats, each arranged in pairs. Thus he found himself sitting alone behind Grégory and Sébastien. While the train started up again slowly towards a great mountain with tumultuous mechanics, Anselme thought of how to start a conversation with Constance. As part of the course, there was a passage buried in total darkness. Everyone screamed except Anselme. Suddenly he heard the voice of a man who seemed to have come into the neighbouring seat.

'What a ride, it shakes!'

He did not answer immediately, his mind wandered so much, he had completely forgotten that nobody took the seat.

'As you say. We must hold on tight!' Anselme nodded politely.

'That was my favorite place. Hold on though, going down's rough!'

'If only that descent could be the sole concern of my day!'

At that moment, just before going out of the darkness, he heard the man's voice laughing, scolding him gently, 'Don't be so stubborn Anselme, and talk to her!'

'Excuse me, who's there?'

They came back to the light of day; Anselme looked at the empty seat and began to wonder if he was not slowly losing his mind.

"That's impossible! He was there! I even felt his presence. I have to going crazy!"

The rollercoaster stopped its dash and prepared to receive new thrill seekers.

The three men got out and joined the women and children.

'Who were you talking to?' asked Grégory.

'I was just thinking out loud,' said Anselme not undering what was happening.

However, he began to add things together. He remembered the foliage in the garden in front of the hotel, that mother calling her son Rémy in the shop at the highway, the billboard with the large eyes, and that nightclub whose logo was a shadow on a lighted background. All of that probably did not have any sense, he thought, but it was nonetheless troubling. An idea suddenly occurred to him, but he refused to admit it. Seeing their return, Kevin suggested that they head to the towering inferno; one of the many other attractions of the park. As in all the rides, many people were in line. Everyone except Anselme joined the queue.

'You're not coming, grandpa?' asked Angel.

He always thought about what he had seen and remained rather evasive. There, Constance decided to break the silence. It was too much.

'Listen,' she said emphatically 'that we are not talking is a fact, but the children did nothing, so you could make an effort for them.'

'That's not it, Constance. I'll tell you later, if you want. Go ahead, I'll wait here.'

He walked away a little not looking back. Constance started worrying, seeing him so far, and turned to her two sons.

'Aside from what you heard this morning, do you know what's going on with him?'

'We thought it was that,' said Sébastien.

'Yes, that morning it wasn't all joyful, but I feel that there are

85

other things.'

'A while ago, I heard him talking when we were at Space Mountain,' clarified Grégory. 'At the time, I thought he was talking to us, but he seemed to talk to someone next to him and I found it downright bizarre.'

'Why?'

'There was no one next to Dad!'

'You're telling me that your father was speaking to himself?'

'Apparently so!'

Increasingly worried, she looked at her husband, not knowing what to think of that sudden change that looked mysterious to her. He seemed to be looking for someone and seemed to be alone in the world.

Suddenly he looked away insistently as if he had a sudden knowledge. Constance was watching and trying to understand. There was no doubt something or someone caught his attention. She looked in turn, but saw nothing but the crowd roaming in all directions. She saw him suddenly run at full speed as if to catch a pickpocket.

'Go on without me,' she said, leaving the queue. She started, trying not to lose sight of that human tide. Who was he following? Anselme would run for noo ne.

Reaching the end of the driveway, he stopped short, looked right and left and passed his hand over his head as if to put his hair in order. Constance joined him a little breathless. Coming to him, she put a hand on his shoulder. He who wasn't easily surprised, was startled as did a fugitive fleeing a predator.

'Honey, what's wrong?' she asked him, surprised and frightened by his attitude.

'I don't know. Strange things have been happening in the past two days.'

'I don't recognize you anymore since we left Saint-Just.'

'I'm afraid, Constance!' he confessed, taking her in his arms.

'Come on, let's go to that bar and tell me everything.'

The couple settled at a table, made their orders and discussed for almost thirty minutes, completely forgetting the rest of the world. His coffee finished, Anselme needed to relieve himself and went down to the toilets. It was just him and the urinals. He positioned himself in front of one of them and relieved himself. He then ran his hands under the water and headed for the exit. At that time, a man, having apparently restrained himself too long, went down urgently and arrived at full speed to the other side of the door. Anselme approached the doorknob and turned it. At that moment, everything happened very quickly. The door suddenly opened and was blocked two inches from his nose. He had instinctively pulled back, and the door, stopped in its tracks, ended its path slowly, as if held back by an invisible force, to the surprise of the two men.

'I'm sorry sir, I wasn't being careful,' said the man convinced that the door was blocked by Anselme's foot!

'No harm done,' he assured, still shocked.

When he joined the table, Constance saw him completely petrified.

'What happened?'

'Let's get out of here and find the others.'

A certain weariness began to wash over. "What does it all mean?" Along the way, he pondered on what happened and he finally drew a conclusion.

"It may be a ghost, a spirit that has been following me from Saint-Just. So, it's true; it exists! And if that's it, whatever it wants from me, it may not be harmful; I could've eaten the door! Whoever you are, I thank you for saving my nose!" At that time, an novel idea crossed his mind. "And if it was... Yes, that's it... A protector... I HAVE A PROTECTOR!"

Constance saw a smile on her husband's face, to her greater stupor, but also to her satisfaction.

Meanwhile, the children had finished with the infernal tower and decided to stay in front of it so as not to confuse Anselme and Constance.

'There they are,' said Grégory, from the top of his six-foot-three height, as such a submarine periscope.

They met halfway. Anselme took the lead and reassured everyone by his reaction. He crouched at the height of his three grand children, and behaved like a real grandfather.

'What do you say to go around the side of The 'Aerosmith'?

'Yeaaaaah !!!!!' shouted the three little ones.

Nobody tried to understand the reasons for that radical change and the rest in the afternoon was enjoyable for the whole family. The children had the time of their lives and even more; the two young couples had fun like children. Anselme had no more visions, nor felt anymore to Constance's joy, who, in addition to the Italian restaurant that had her recall fond memories, forgot that disastrous morning.

12

Florentine maneuvers

'It's almost always, in a family,
that a dreamer carries it through.'
Gabrielle Roy

Six o'clock struck and Constance was worried about the dinner they were invited to. She had no difficulties in convincing the children who had not stopped all day to go to the hotel to prepare. They were exhausted and there was a strong chance that they will fall asleep during the performance. Constance did not exactly know what to expect in the evening, but she was the only one to knew a bit more than everyone else.

'You want to tell me where we're going tonight or is it too early?' questioned Anselme whose curiosity was growing.

She looked at him, smiling.

'It's a concert,' she said, with a touch of mystery.

Anselme stomped with impatience.

'Okay... whose concert?'

'That, I don't know, but I know you'll like it!'

'And that's far away? Because it's already six!'

'No, it's just nearby...'

'Yeah... I got it!'

'So let's waste no more time and go to the hotel to change!'

Anselme liked surprises, but it has been two days since he was held in secret. It was too much! Everyone around him knew or strongly suspected to be what it was. He thought of a possible subtle means to finally know what was coming. He decided thus to change in less time than it took to tell, and joined the others who were waiting in the lobby.

'You have an appointment?' joked Constance.

'I just want to eat something before we go; a sandwich will do nicely. Unless that's included in your planning?'

She could see that that was a final attempt to learn more.

'Don't worry, we have it covered!'

'In that case, I'll wait downstairs with the children,' he continued giving Constance a kiss on the forehead, who chuckled inwardly. "If only you knew, darling."

He took the elevator and arrived in the great hall. He headed straight for the guy who was there to receive customers.

'Good evening, sir,' he said, wearing a calculated relaxation.

'Good evening, sir,' replied the employee with a smile.

Knowing her husband 'by heart', Constance had spread the word to the employees, with the help of tips, to remain silent on the course of the evening, whatever happens by preparing them, that he might be able of all the tricks to get any information.

'Tonight we're dining out, we won't be eating here, but perhaps you already know, Anselme ventured very seriously.

'Yes Sir, your wife informed us this morning,' answered the employee, a little amused.

"Ouch," thought Anselme, "she thought of everything!"

Anselme adopted a smug expression and settled in front of the counter as wuld a cowboy in a saloon.

'Tonight we're going to the concert, which w is not far from here, you know...'

'Ah, no sir; please pardon me, I am not very interested in musical events.'

'How could a young man like you not be interested in music?'

'No sir, I did not say that, I'm just saying I'm not interested in musical events!'

"At your age, I won't be holding back!"

Anselme gave up and joined the group in concluding...

'But you should!'

He tried his luck one last time with the doorman who was heading towards the entrance, and opted that time for a jovial behavior.

'Hello Sir, beautiful evening isn't it!'

The employee stared at the door a few moments.

'Indeed it is!'

Anselme did not feel bold enough to tell him about the concert and preferred to give up. Realising that he would have been more successful in 'beating a dead horse', he turned and joined the others.

'Good luck to you, boy.' "They all spread the word that's incredible!"

'Thank you sir, good evening!' the employee replied, winking twice.

Seeing that, Anselme gad a moment of hesitation, and then continued toward his children. At that moment, he heard the same voice he had heard at the rides in Disneyland...

"Patience...!"

Here, everyone in the hall could see him look around him, looking for someone.

'Easy to sa...' Noticing he spoke alone, he stopped.

"My poor children, I think that your old dad' definitely losing it," he said to himself, looking into their direction.

Sébastien and Grégory stared silently; it was the second time they saw him like that and began to ask questions about the mental health of their father.

When Constance came into the hall, wearing a splendid dress covered by a beautiful fur coat, she saw everyone's eyes on her husband. "What has he done now!"

Anselme felt the weight of the stares on him. If he could fold himself over to fit in his pocket, he would have very willingly done so already.

The whole family was assembled and ready to go.

'Is all well?' asked Constance joining the grou.

'Yes, don't worry,' said Anselme embarrassed, 'I still found a way to stand out!'

'That's what I thought I saw!

'You're stunning sweetheart.

'Thank you... It's for you!'

'Really... So let me take a photo and go change,' he joked; 'I don't want to have to fight to keep you by my side tonight!'

'Pinch me I'm dreaming,' said Constance charmed, 'you just complimented me!'

The couple looked into each other's eyes like two lovebirds.

It was touching to see them; especially after that long day of mutual ignorance.

Anselme had that 'tongue-in-cheek' side to him as well as does his daughter in law Sofia, whom he particularly appreciated for that singularity.

Thus, he did not hesitate to go from Point A to Point B.

'I'm hungry, so let's go grab some drive through on the way?'

At that moment, everyone looked at each other. Everything was perfect... except for the meal! They forgot to 'prepare' Anselme at the idea that they would eat at "Burg's-Resto" on the way to the stadium.

But Constance was ready, knowing very well that it was Anselme's type of establishment, and that honesty is the best policy. She therefore adopted a more playful attitude to tell him.

'Given the little time we have left, we decided to to please the children and to eat at Burg's-Resto which is on the way to the stadium,' she said, using her fatal weapon of lovingly calculated seduction, "Don't fuss, and say, YES." 'That's alright with you, darling?' All was packaged with a smile.

His reaction was rather lively...

'AT BURG'S-RESTO! You knew very well that it never appealed to me, so might as well buy rat poison and take a sip each. That way, we know exactly what we'll die of!'

'Anselme!' Constance snapped, 'the children...!'

It composed himself and called himself a 'Formula 1 Driver getting ready to drive his car with a pedal than with an engine:

'Your grandmother, uh... your old grandmother's right, we'll have a great time at "Good Old Burg's",' he said sarcastically.

'You'll never change,' says Constance upset by the situation, 'are you sixty-nine or nineteen?'

Despite the guns that were pointed from her retinas, he 'behaved' and remained silent up to the entrance of the restaurant. The other members of the group were silent and the children already savoured in thinking of their 'Cheese Burg's'.

Upon arrival, after walking for about ten minutes they went to settle at a table. To be certain of what he will be eating, Anselme proposed to order along with this grandchildren.

'Sit down, I'll take care of everything! So it's there we'll go,' he said, pointing to the counter...

'Yes, Anselme,' said Véronique smelling an imminente disaster.

THE DAY MY SOUL SPOKE

'Would you like me to come with you? I'm used to these places, since the kids love it so much…'

'If you want to, my dear, but I am quite capable of ordering some burgers and fries!'

'I don't doubt for a moment Anselme, but once you see what children want, you won't regret that I came…'

'Of course, so let's go.'

Constance said nothing, but she already laughed inwardly, just imagine the head that he would do when he actually sees the famous sandwiches.

While Anselme, his daughter in law and children waited for their turn, Constance, her two sons and Sofia discussed.

'Do you think he'll manage to get by with all those burgers?' asked Sébastien to his mother.

'Is this the first time in a Burg's-Resto?' added Grégory, 'I pity the cashier…'

'Don't worry about your father, when he's hungry, he understands quickly and well!'

'You speak of him as if he's a big eater,' marvelled Sofia, amused in hear them.

'We're just laughing at him,' said Constance, 'but there's still some truth. While working at the clinic, the meal was one of the best times of the day because some days were very stressful, and when he ate, it was a cherished moment; he thought of nothing else. To top it all off, he is a true gourmet. That's why we had fun, because having him wait and stand before the counter of the food he hates must be a real ordeal for him. But fortunately, the children are here, and he's able to make huge sacrifices for them… As he did for you, boys,' she concluded, looking at her sons.

Suddenly Sofia's phone rang. She took it out from her bag and picked up.

'Hello... Mom... yes, you're at the stadium... Yes, I'll ask...'

'Who should they look for at the stadium's entrance?'

'They must show their invitations and say "Mickael Fournier" is expecting them. And normally they should be lead to the seats reserved for us.

Sofia repeated instructions to the letter to her mother, then hung up.

'They're not lost, are they?' asked Constance.

'No, they wonder just what was going to happen tonight, but knowing the fact that it's in honor of Anselme reassures them.'

'Too bad that Véronique's parents were unable to make it, it we would allowed us to get to know each other better.

During that time, the person who ordered before Anselme, Véronique and the children, had a hard time choosing his hamburgers and took a lot of time to decide. While the server tried expedite the movement, explaining the ingredients contained in the 'cheeseburg's' and other 'fishburg's', Anselme was becoming seriously impatient.

'This one has Merlot with salad leaves and tomatoes... would you like that one?'

'Hmmm... Yes... Uh no wait t... Do you have one with spicy meat?

'Of course; we have the "Texaswalkerrocker", would you rather have that?'

'YES, HE WOULD VERY MUCH RATHER!' Anselme was highly exasperated.

All eyes were on him; he understood that then he certainly should not have had to be carried away.

'Sorry ma'am,' he said, trying to ease the mood, but my

grandchildren are starving!

Véronique could not believe her ears. How could he dare?

'Please... Anselme... Calm down!'

But the children approved.

'Yeah, grandpa, c'mon, you show 'em!' the kids proudly said.

Although the situation was becoming embarrassing for him,

It did accelerate the indecisive person to set his sights on the 'Cheeseburg's'.

Having been on the verge of being considered 'the evening's kill-joy,' he was at that point relegated to the rank of 'Nice Old Geezer', who must be served as soon as possible to avoid making a scene at the store.

The line finally freed up and they moved forward.

'Hello, friend,' said Anselme, as would a famished conquistador dismounting his horse after winning a battle. 'I am listening!'

The server had a moment of confusion.

'Good evening sir, madam; you're listening to me, you said?'

'Yes, young man, what do you suggest?'

Displaying a discreet smile and collecting all the patience he had in stock, he pointed to the light panels, above his head where everything was listed.

'Everything's written here, sir, but I see that you're not used to this, so I'll help you out...'

He enumerated some of the available sandwiches and explained what he was entitled according to the menu he would be taking. Anselme, was soon lost in all that 'Mic-Mac' of hamburgers, fries, potatoes and other nuggets.

In the end, he passed the baton to Véronique, who did it with so much amusement that it was as if a Super Banana was painted on her face from the left ear to the right ear, just to see the successive expressions face Anselme exhibited since the beginning, as he tried to understand.

Knowing how to fill the children in a fast food, it did not take long to place the order for everyone, including that of Anselme, who had given up.

The server was beginning to fill the tray with the first burgers that were ready, and the first batch of fries. Anselme could not take his eyes in those little 'waxed cardboard' boxes, each of which contained a sandwich.

"That's it, their hamburger?" He thought, already thinking of a solution to have more, without being noticed.

At that point, the survival instinct took over...

'Excuse me young man, would you please add six more burgers in case anyone is still not satisfied, and please, a bottle of red wine.'

The server and Véronique had both understood that the only person who had the best chance not to be had was him and him alone.

'Of course sir... Six more burgers are on the way, but for the wine...'

Véronique interrupted the server to relieve him of that explanation.

'There's no wine here Anselme, only soft drinks!'

'Why did I even ask!' he said, shaking his head.

Anselme was certainly not fond of the food, but the smell of cooked meat, fries and all that came from the kitchen, however, had managed to whet his appetite.

Looking at his daughter in law from the corner of his eye, he noticed that she was gently mocking him. He thought fit to add a ladle and thus sank more...

'Don't you agree, Véronique that the children can still be hungry after that Feast-Menu...'

'Of course Anselme, you are absolutely right and it's very wise of you to thinking about that,' she nodded with friendly smile.

At that moment, he realized that what he had to do was to shut up permanently.

Suddenly he saw through the kitchen shelves where the burgers were stored, a young man of thirty years old, who seemed to have Rémy's features, with curly brown hair, that Brad Pitt face with eyes he had often seen open and in close up. He decided not to react, but he could not help but follow with his gaze.

Suddenly, the man who seemed to give orders, suddenly approached the shelves with big open hazel eyes, to see everyone in the room. He did it so quickly and so soon, Anselme had the impression he was going through.

Surprised and taken aback, he had a back reaction, then pulled himself together.

"It won't happen again," he thought.

However, it did not bother him. Far from being frightened, he was curious, he wanted to knew what exactly was going on. Mais for the time-being, he had to focus on one thing: eat and go to this concert, hitherto the source of all these mysteries.

'What's happening, Anselme?' asked Véronique who noticed his frozen "disconnection" before the cash register.

He looked straight ahead, without even responding to the server, who finished serving their food. He did not even care about what Véronique was saying, he was so obsessed with what he saw.

Constance noticed the scene and immediately thought of what he had told her in the bar where the toilet had proved a perilous adventure for him. Worried, she started to get up to join him, and in the interest of not wanting to panic anyone, she sat back own.

'It's okay, mom,' said Sébastien cutting the momentum of his mother with a a reassuring gesture, 'I'll go help them bring the trays.'

Hiding her worry, she nodded.

Having recovered from his emotion, Anselme took a tray filled with several servings of fries and walked to their table with the children. Véronique had offered to pay for everything and wrapped up with the server, when Sébastien arrived to take one of the two remaining sets.

'Here are the burgers,' said Sébastien arriving with the tray, Véronique following with the drinks.

Constance looked at her husband who was beginning to open the packaging, but he did not really look disgusted and that reassured her.

Véronique finally arrived with the soft drinks without any sign of the red wine. She put the tray on the table, settled in and having had no answer, repeated her question to Anselme.

'What was going on at the counter? It was like you've seen a ghost.'

'That's exactly right,' he said in the tone of the joke, at the same time avoiding all unnecessary explanations.

Anxious not to spoil the evening, he preferred to open up a little, hoping not to have to say everything.

'I just thought I saw someone I know, and when you talked to me, I was trying to see his face better, that's all. I'm sorry if I didn't answer you right away.'

'Don't mention it, Anselme,' she said, starting to unwrap her "Cheeseburg's".

Constance quietly watched her stubborn husband became ultimately reasonable. It looked more like him; she was relieved.

The evening had a chance again to be successful.

All began to help themselves once Anselme did want to be seen as what he was… The children threw themselves on what they chose, the women paid attention to their figures and went through their meals slowly. Sébastien and Grégory, their father's sons, had in the corner of their eyes, the six additional burgers that their father had ordered 'just in case' and hastened to eat so as to be among the first to seconds.

'These hamburgers were quickly devoired!' said Anselmeen chewing his last bite. 'Fortunately, there are extra because it's not with just that, that we'll survive the evening!'

'You're absolutely right Dad,' said Grégory mouth still full, grabbing another burger. Sébastien quickly did the same when he saw the precious sandwiches disappear at Mach speed.

'And none's left for the dogs,' Constance said gently. 'Have you asked the children if they still want more?'

Hand on what he hoped to be his third serving, Anselme changed his mind and asked the question to the children.

'Yes grandpa, it's so good!' cried toddlers.

He tried to hide his disappointment, but it showed so much on his face, that Constance could not help teasing him.

'Dogs can't meow, darling,' she said ironically, pointedly looking at the hamburgers still held captive in his hands, at the little ones all as gluttonous as their fathers and grandfather.'

'I'm going to order three more and come right back,' he said, beginning to stand.

'Anselme, you've already finished two and as many servings of fries by yourself; besides, it's already past seven, and we don't have much time. Also, the shuttle that goes to the stadium will arrive soon and the next comes in after another half hour, so please…'

'You're probably right sweetie and I have to watch my weight anyway!'

Everyone had almost finished his meal. Only Kevin, Gérémi and Angel still had a bite or two left.

13

Who are you?

'As you get older, you learn to trade
your terrors against sneers.'
Emil Cioran Michel

Then everyone began to prepare to leave, the Shuttle
appeared at the bus stop.
'Crap!' said Grégory, jumping up urgently, 'We gotta
go, the shuttle's here!' Putting on his coat hastily, he continued in
his momentum… 'I'll tell him to wait a bit,' and he went rushing
in the shuttle's direction.

His right arm still in the air, he literally took with him a man
and his tray without stopping…

'Excuse me, no more time!' said the tall son who became a
cannonball!

'Ouch!' said Sébastien as he helped Sofia and Véronique dress
the kids.

"And who will take care of picking up the pieces?" Anselme
thought strongly

'Leave it, dad,' said Sébastien going towards the unlucky man,
'I'll do it…'

They rose and pressed towards the exit at a run, to reach

the place where the bus was parked two hundred meters away. Sébastien approached the area and tried to apologize to the man who seemed to carry the misery of the world on his shoulders. But the icy stare that he got prompted Sébastien to take out a bill from his wallet which amounted to twice what was only slimy mess on the floor.

'I'm really sorry, sir,' he humbly said, 'we really have no more time; just punch me in the face after the concert, ok?'

The man chuckled quietly and then said with controlled wisdom.

'Leave quickly and have a good concert!'

Sébastien could not believe his ears.

'Thank you...'

'Save it, sonny, I already want to wring your neck!'

The young man said simply nodded... "Message received!"

While Grégory ran with all he had towards the shuttle before it went away, screaming with all his might 'Wait, don't go!,' he suddenly saw the shuttle begin moving, then stop just as fast.

"He saw me," he thought, relieved.

The driver, who had not seen or heard anything, attempted a second start, which ended in a second failure.

"What's he doing?" Grégory wondered.

The driver did not seem to understand what was happening.

The third test was successful, just when Grégory, out of breath, came up to the bus. Surprised, the driver finally opened the door.

'Forgive me, I didn't see you. But apparently today's your lucky day, sir, because if the engine had not stalled twice, you would have had to wait for my colleague who will be here in half an hour.'

'I wondered what you were doing,' said Grégory, explaining what he had seen. 'I'm not alone, he said, there are still seven who are coming.'

'Rest assured Sir, now that I saw you I will wait, and I will not move!'

When the rest of the family arrived Anselme thanked the driver for his kindness.

'It's not me you should thank, but the bus!'

'The bus?'

'I didn't see you,' said the man, and if it hadn't been stubborn when I wanted to start, I would've left without you. The only thing that bothers me about this is that we just brought it, and that this darned thing's brand new! We'll have to see the dealers after only three days of use; they no longer make them like they used to, and that's a shame, believe me!'

'It shouldn't be a big deal,' ventured Anselme, seeking to reassure the driver.

'No, I don't think so, especially since it has worked very well until this evening or rather, until it saw you coming... I think you scared it!' joked the driver who seemed to be light-hearted enough for a few laughs.

At that moment, a thought crossed Anselme's mind, a strange thought... Constance immediately understood what he had in mind.

"So you're still here," he thought, casting a furtive glance on the bus' ceiling. "Again, thank you..."

'I will present my apologies once we head down, I promise,' he said to the driver, jokingly.

The man smiled, closed the door and started up. Anselme took his seat beside Constance, made himself comfortable and sighed, as if to evacuate an 'overflow'.

'I don't know what's happening, but I'll find out. Clearly, he's just in time!'

'There certainly are some "bad spirits" who mess up your life, and apparently "protectors" too, who make it wonderful,' Constance ventured.

'Maybe I'm developping the ability to communicate with ghosts, who knew? The most frustrating for me is that communication's one way; if you can call it a communication. Up until then, he does me favours and I thank him! That's what it boils down to.'

Constance looked at him lovingly and took his hand to remind him of her presence at his side.

He looked in turn, smiled and concluded with those words, before getting lost in thought.

'Me too.'

"What are you? A ghost, a spirit, an energy, maybe all in one… maybe my imagination's growing; or do I just have such an incredible opportunity these last few days! If you really exist and that my neurons are still in place, who are you? Show yourself, give me a sign; I also want to help you, or even talk to you… Whatever you are, or whoever you are, I WANT TO KNOW YOU!"

From his 'aisle seat', he looked straight ahead, through the windshield; the landscape flew by and the planted streetlights along the entire path seemed to be there to 'introduce' the powerful lights of the site where the concert was to take place. But suddenly something caught his attention, something on the edge of the road. It looked like a glow, much like a ray of light without a clear form. It seemed to accompany them, but outside leading them from one hundred and fifty meters away. It did not walk, nor ran, but seemed rather fly in the airs, floating. It looked at Constance and the others, but no one seemed to see it. Continuing to observe silently in the dark of the night, regularly punctuated by the streetlights which highlighted it even more between each post, he was the only one to see it; it stood still, and then went off again like a kindly escort. Anselme did not let it out of his sight, he was fascinated.

"Ah… there you are, he thought. But, do not just stay outside, come in and introduce yourself!"

He suddenly saw the shape disappear full speed.

The bus was not far from the stadium. At that time, Sébastien called out, saying that he would certainly appreciate the musical evening.

There Anselme realized he there were too many people around for him to establish a 'contact'.

'Celtic?' he ventured, turning to his son.

'Yes, everything you love, Dad!'

'It will surely be a good evening,' he concluded, turning, always thinking of his ray of light.

"OK, I understood. Later then!"

14

Welcome...

'When silence is speech and speech is silence,
the front door of the gift is freely opened.'
Marcel Aymé

The shuttle soon arrived near the stadium entrance where an extremely dense crowd was already present.

Seeing that, Anselme already felt his legs go sore, nothing but imagining the long wait; "We will be there for at least an hour!"

'We're not out of the woods yet,' remarked Grégory, not too enthusiastically.

They went down the bus and headed to the cashier.

Constance noticed a family that came along with them. She was sure she knew; she had already seen them in... Saint-Just? Perhaps, or from the surrounding area. Apparently better informed, they headed directly for one of the security guards, who, after having exchanged a few words, took their tickets by indicating where they should. Constance quietly observed them. They were entitled to a personal escort, having presented what appeared to be an invitation similar to those they had received; so it was sensible to think that he can do the same for them.

'Give me all your invitations and follow me,' she ordered as such would a battalion commander in an evening dress.

'Yes chief!' joked Sébastien, holding out their invitation at attention.

The clan did as the 'model family' and arrived at one of the agents. All had special instructions for Anselme and his family as the 'guest of honour'. Michael, the organizer of the evening, took care to show a photograph of Anselme ordering special treatment for him, and his companions.

The officer asked them to please wait a moment, took his cell phone and advised the head of their arrival, who arrived in just five minutes to personally welcome them.

'Oh, you are finally here,' he said, warmly shaking their hands, 'Did you have a good trip? My name was Michael Fournier, I'm the producer of this show, but call me "Michael"! Follow me,' said the man who appeared to be impressed by Anselme, 'I will escort you personally.'

Astonished at that reception, Anselme followed suit. He led them directly to their seats located just in front of the stage in the middle of the row in which some of their families were already seated, as were much of those from the village and towns neighbouring Saint-Just.

"What were they doing here?" He thought, seeing all those familiar faces. Anselme and his beloved who supported him, politely waved to those they recognized.

As they walked, Michael started a brief conversation with Anselme, because time mattered to him.

'They told me much about you, I would almost say that I know you already, even if we have only seen each other for the first time!'

'Who told you so much about me like that?'

'That... I do not have the right to tell you, but I knew you were an excellent nurse and you were as a musician in your free time!'

'You were fully informed until then!'

'Do you continue to play or was it all in the past?'

'More than ever, now that I have all the time...'

Michael looked at him, outlining a broad smile thinking probably what was intended for him.

'You're right, Anselme... uh, may I just call you Anselme?'

'Of course, Michael...'

Everyone looked at the setup, the scene, the lighting, people sitting in their seats; everything was so great.

'We're here,' said Michael showing them with his left hand nine places. 'Do pardon me, but I still have quite a lot of work to do. Have a good evening and see you later...'

'Thank you, Michael. See you later.'

At that time, he had a moment of astonishment.

'See you later...? Why did he say that?' he asked, turning to Constance.

'I don't know, he had to be wrong... He must have so many details to think about, it was even surprising that he escorted us!'

But it must be related to those invitations we received...

15

Final adjustments

'When you're confused, free yourself. When awake, every-thing is there.'
Adam Mickiewicz

Meanwhile the musicians, rehearsing since the day before, were getting ready for the show. All had stage fright, but they all shared one motivation: surprise their families, their friend Anselme and with a little luck, the audience...

But for now, a battle took place backstage. Even if one believed in the success of a project, the producer cannot help thinking about the singularity of the evening; it was a first in the field and there still would be a risk that that the event could not appreciated at its true value.

Nicole has assumed more or less, in spite of herself, the leader's hat and reviewed the musicians, the choristers and the singers. She started with the ringers...

'Everyone, remember that it's on the fourteenth that everyone can actually see what we have accomplished. Do you remember which one?'

Having rehearsed many times, Pascal, one of the joyous fellows of the troupe, sighed and replied, 'Yes, we remember, it's on Mireille Mathieu's "Yes, I think" where we proudly show the result of our work!'

It caused a wave of laughter to go over the group, and Nicole kindly shot him down with a look. But those few words successfully relaxed everybody, and not to annoy Nicole who was already stressed, Romain continued by reassuring her.

'"The Brendan Theme". Do not worry, we'll nail it.'

"Yes, we'll make it," she thought, contemplating their faces. She smiled and continued her inspection.

'And you, Sylvestre?'

'On the last guitar note, surprise!'

'OK; Kevin?'

'We'll go around him and make him the show's prisoner!'

'Good. Now, listen to me, all of you. No one will doubt over anything prior to the fourteenth, got it?'

Everyone agreed with a nod and replied in chorus, as a group of young school children.

"Yes, NICOOOLE!"

Stress started a break, leaving room for a kind of courage that generated confidence and aplomb acquired throughout reconstructive walkthrough. Thanking them from bottom of her heart, she continued with a refreshed tone.

'We'll show them!'

It was now 7:50 p.m., and for them, it there was more than an hour and a half before it all began. Michael, producer and patron of the show, had come with his own team for lighting, sound and video engineers for the giant screen that stood fifteen meters long and ten meters high. The concert would be worthy of the greatest spectacles. Everything was there:

• A sumptuous decor that showed two ranges of giant music

notes, disposed on each side of the screen.

• On the stage measuring ninety meters long and forty meters wide were willing several levels with stairs which formed a large circle.

• In the centre, on the highest level, a complete battery was installed.

• At each end of the stage two huge column speakers had been erected, providing a total capacity of twenty thousand watts.

• A multitude of projectors, strobes and other light effects were set high above the musicians. Some were even at the centre of the stage where four people were perched, governing the sound and lighting.

And to top it all, no fewer than fourteen thousand people would attend the concert to which everyone would have seated places. To attract the crowd, organizers had taken the decision not to reveal everything. Posters were published en masse, and television and radio commercials announced a formation of Celtic musicians, sponsored by the biggest names in the genre. The seats were paid, but the price was not excessive.

16

One small step for us...

*'Music is a higher revelation
than all wisdom and philosophy.'*
Ludwig Van Beethoven

The big moment came fast. All the spectators were there. Bernard, Suzanne and Sofia's parents had been welcomed in the same way that the guests in the front row where they belonged to their great amazement.

Thirteen seats were reserved for them on the first row. Upon seeing his friends, Anselme worried for Drakkar.

'How is it that you're here? Did you come with the dog, or did you decide to let him starve to death?'

'Don't worry, Yannick's home to take care of him.'

'I didn't know you too were interested in Celtic music.'

'To tell you the truth, we didn't know either!'

'I don't understand.'

'Don't bother. If we understand correctly, you'll have the answer tonight.'

Anselme frowned and sat back in his seat. "Nicole's Band" still had time to mentally prepare. So as not to 'bluff' the fans of Celtic music, Michael had decided to call on the most famous for the first part, such as Gilles Servat, Prigent or even Alan Stivell who had accepted terms just as easily as others would for a just cause in their eyes. That was certainly not the usual procedure, but in a representation that Michael mistakenly thought unique, nothing would be usual.

8:45 p.m., the lights started to illuminate the scene that was, up to that time, kept in the dark. The public brouhaha gradually faded, and that was when Sharon Shannon opening the ball by singing 'Sandy River Bell.' She will be followed by Denez Prigent, Alan Stivell, Gilles Servat, Rita Connolly, Baghdad Laun Bihoué and Shaun Davey.

All fans were ecstatic, and Michael and rubbed his hands. It was then that they were going to have to show some open-mindedness he thought, trying to hide his apprehension. Gilles Servat, who has always had that ease on stage, has agreed to take the microphone to introduce his new friends to the public. It was to introduce a new genre of musicians, not a band of handicapped people. The task was a bit tricky, but not impossible. For their part, Nicole, Victor, Pascal and others who had been impressed by all the vastness upon setting their eyes the stadium, the stage and the materials, they were finally ready, even if deep inside them, they were dying of stage fright.

"Ladies and gentlemen, exceptions do not occur every day. We have come to know people worthy of that title, and we all fall in love."

At that time, other distinguished guests who had sung since the beginning of the concert, joined him as to give more weight to his words. After a moment of surprise, he continued.

"Tonight the music we all love will take on a new dimension. I ask you to welcome as it should be, a one of a kind band, 'La

Troupe Méribell.'"

While he was speaking, a film appeared on the giant screen, showing the old clinical from a bird's eye view while the first musicians came on stage in a wheelchair, following an accurate route and in order of arrival previously established. They were a fifty who poured in with the audience's applause. Anselme gaped and could not contain his emotion rising and applauding with all his might. Everyone was there; he recognized them all. The surprise was complete. "This is my gift!" He looked at his wife, children and friends by displaying a smile of fulfilment and recognition.

'Thank you for keeping the secret, I was not expecting it at all.' He was beginning to regret the stupid reaction he had at the hotel with his beloved, but the experience he was undergoing overcame everything else. Tonight was here!

Constance looked at him with love and mouthed the words, "I love you".

Anselme focused again on the show, impatient and excited to see them play. It was Nicole who was about to begin. She approached the microphone, looked at 'Le Clan Anselme' with a satisfied smile, and all of the families of musicians and singers sitting in first three rows, in their pockets the same invitation as Anselme's. The first instruments began to hum the notes a song called 'Borders of Salt' sung originally by Dan An Braz. They had made no original piece since they did not intend to get a place in the Celtic musical landscape. True, they had all become able to play and sing with the greatest, but it was not the purpose of the operation. Tonight they would simply flourish and accomplish, in front of those most dear to their hearts.

So, Nicole began her singing with ease like a pop star. Everyone could hear her crystalline and melodious voice. Now, no one had

115

stage fright anymore, all systems go!

A film still showed on the giant screen, showing their evolution throughout the years. They had taken care to film themselves to remember, and when the time comes that the only magic intervened in their feat was simply their unwavering motivation. Anselme and the public had before their eyes practically all of the people he had taken care of from 1988 to 1994. All worked hard, doing physical exercises, each one especially hounding their disability. Some trained, others practiced with their musical instruments. Soon, others were seen.

Victor trying to tame his bagpipes. Jérôme whose left arm was severely damaged in a car accident, work on acoustic guitar pieces.

Jean-Luc, a big blond Viking-like man whose left hand was partly rebuilt, pounding on drums.

Damien enjoyed his electric guitar while everyone else had condemned his right arm. He was the life and soul of the band. He was seen indulging from time to time traveling the hangar to and fro with his mad guitar, as did the Angus Youg of AC/DC. Some smiled, others got upset and seemed to want him to tie the knot. That was not to displease Éric, whenever he was seen indulging in his passions, accompanying him in rhythm with his bass.

Bertrand's taunts were seen as well, one of sixteen ringers and the most cantankerous of the group, break down several times when things became too hard for him.

Just a few shocking images were shown in which the percussionists suffered some damage to their faces.

Leah was amputated on her right leg and had moments of depression.

Sylvestre, a man of five-feet-four, made up for his height by wanting to stand out as he yelled about everything! He was also the only one who was annoyed with Anselme at the time. But even if he was missing half of his left leg, despite his infernal character, he had found the motivation to control his flute like Carlos Nuñez, a virtuoso in the matter, he was a fan.

Nicole had lost her right forearm and was constantly depressed in the early days of her disability. But today, against all odds, she kicks them in the butt when she saw someone moping or angry at someone when they did not do their work well. Those who knew her discovered a person who had the will to win and who, standing on her five-feet-seven, with her brown hair in a square cut and fine but very expressive features, lead her little group with her baton!

Anselme was disappointed seeing Sylvestre on those images... "At least they could've managed to stuff something in his beak to make him stop!"

But there was no malice in his heart. He smiled and was admiring them. He watched them, studied them with great attention. All had progressed despite their disability. Most of those who were in a wheelchair managed to get up, some even walked with more or less ease. Others used walkers or crutches, and some managed to walk unaided, but carefully. Those images showed ten years of effort, the best and the most difficult moments. Their relatives, who had suspected nothing all that time, understood everything now. When they returned home, they would resettle in their armchairs, so as no longer to move! That was also part of their motivation; they counted well to be physically ready to achieve that result. What could be more motivating!

Anselme was completely disconnected from the rest of the crowd, as he were on another planet, lost in thought.

"It's true, I've made you part of my own experience, but I never pushed you to get into music. I agree that it's better to play standing rather than sitting, but you could occupy yourself with anything else, as long as it's close to your heart. But here is a concert worthy of Mick Jagger!"

Regardless, the screen was not big enough to contain their will; they believed and it showed. It was almost palpable. All these musicians were unusual but the results were there.

"There were some things that were best done alone..."

Some have even taken a work rhythm coming from that hangar, as if they were going to work somewhere else, while others fought hard to annihilate their disability, while participating in their musical project. One could see clearly the focus with which they worked. Like real professionals, everything was calculated to the second during rehearsals; settled like music paper. There was no way for them to announce such an event and then make an awkward show to make people laugh, who certainly would be there for the show, but also there to judge their performance. They wanted to show the world that the will and motivation, everything can happen.

For families who discovered, together with everyone else, that their husband, their wife, their brother, their sister, or their child, it was clear when they found themselves at the entrance of the stadium that something unusual was going to happen that evening. In addition, all members of the band had found an excuse not to attend. Already, the simple fact of having them play in such a show gave them a collective pride, doubled by a mixture of admiration and joy, but it was there, the beginning of the show of the 'Méribell' band.

In the first song that Nicole sang in English, late eloquent words were sung at the: 'It's all to you'; everyone could interpret as they like. It was by opening her arms wide and displaying a wide smile she sang those words directly addressing families, but also to Anselme, who was amazed by what he saw. "They really thought of everything"; he noticed the backrests of the chairs of the ringers who had been lowered for the movement of their arms. He thought, "After all, professionalism in business, whatever it is, is to leave nothing to chance."

When she finished her song, she made it known to everyone, that there was someone she knew, who gave them the urge to go forward; a person able to understand better than anyone, the constraints of a wheelchair, or finding oneself deprived with the use of a limb. She stared looked at Anselme pointedly... "Come, come with us," her eyes said; she held out her hand to him, inviting him to join them on the stage, in order to bring them all together in front of the giant screen which was broadcast from the beginning of her speech, images and film clips taken from the clinic. Patients there were indeed filmed twenty-four-seven in their rooms to alert staff of any problems. But there was also the last days of Rémy, who had also, in his own way, given them hope. Seeing that, Anselme could no longer hold back, and he let go completely and wept bitterly as he headed for all those people, who were waiting for him to receive the greatest gift in the world.

Ringers began a piece, 'The Brendan Theme' from Shaun Davey. The moment he put a first foot on the boards, the magic began; all who were sitting on their chairs stood up and some began to walk toward him, while continuing to play their instruments with great pride. Others, with larger lesions, had to move with a walker, remained standing for a few moments in front of their chair and then sat down again. But it was already a great achievement for them; the fruit of many years of work and suffering. They all looked pointedly at him, watching for his reactions.

At that moment, was displayed on the screen in big letters, "THANK YOU AND MERRY CHRISTMAS".

The excitement was at its height. Fourteen thousand spectators were all standing; they applauded not only the show, but also the lesson of humanity for the price of a single concert. For Anselme, he no longer realised he was crying. It was simply magical. They circled him, and they all turned towards the screen where the images Rémy continued playing.

What Anselme had felt, the day in which he rose from his wheelchair by himself chair in front of Constance, became dwarfed by what he felt that night with them.

Everyone was moved; for them to give him that wonderful gift, the public were still standing, continuing to applaud their families, everyone as speechless as Anselme who, as cherry on the cake, could see himself at his friend's company Rémy winking, when he took care of him. It was really intense. Before closing his eyes for good, Rémy had confided to a person as sensitive as Anselme of some particular mission. He secretly communicated telepathically with Nicole; he had asked her to write a few words from him to them and to Anselme. Nicole did not understand those words at the time, but she still kept them carefully noted and had realised their meaning over the years, especially that night. They would be be displayed on the giant canvas, over his face seen in close-up; they said:

"Tonight, the music has helped to make you worthy of the feelings that your family feel about you and to show everyone that anything is possible.

You who have been my only family, and you Anselme, who came to bid me 'good night' every night before going home, had been a great comfort to me. Do not mourn my death, laugh at it, because I am very happy where I am today; so if you wish to, Anselme, my friend, you can bid me 'good night' one last time."

The movie ended with music when Rémy closed his eyes. Jérôme walked towards Anselme and held out his acoustic guitar.

"This is part of your gift with a song that you know quite well."

'But that's my guitar!'

Jérôme smiled, proud to have been chosen for that role. Anselme cried like a madeleine and had no more room for stage fright. He did not take long to understand. He took the guitar, while Sylvestre approached him, flute in hand. Both settled down, willing to maintain the magic of the evening with music by Carlos Núñez playing 'St. Patrick An Dro' after everyone had taken their places back onstage.

"Who knew those two would end one day end up onstage in front of such a crowd!"

Both sat each on a chair in front of the scene. Initially, Sylvestre played virtually alone, punctuated by Damien at the end of each verse. Then gradually Anselme's came in, in perfect harmony with Sylvestre. What came out of that flute/acoustic guitar duet was simply beautiful, especially Anselme, who played not as regularly as he did before, he did not miss a single note. By the time they had finished their piece, the ringers sitting lined up behind the duo took over to close the song. Armed with his flute, Sylvestre rose in turn and reached out to Anselme, inviting him to walk toward the front of the stage a few meters from the spectators. There was no more to be done than to be transported by the magic permanently set on the scene, and in the twenty-eight thousand eyes fixed on him. Sylvestre was limping a little, but no matter, he did not even think about it. Anselme had put both feet in that parallel world for a night; he was part of the troupe; he was thrilled. Families still cannot get over the constancy manifested by the task and the ability to keep their secret against all odds; they were stunned and filled with happiness. Constance felt immense pride, just like her sons and grandchildren. Sofia, her parents and Véronique were in awe of this 'little man', humble and discreet and who spoke rarely of his past and they discovered a humanity never seen before. As for his lifelong friends Bernard and Suzanne, they knew him and appreciated those qualities at their fair value. But that did not prevent them from being stunned in front of that grandiose show they had the chance to experience, all before a conquered and wondrous audience.

On the right and on the left of the giant screen, well above of the band, were lit the towering notes "DO-RE-MI" and on the same screen was displayed:

"DORS RÉMY et BONNE NUIT" – "Sleep, Rémy and good night."

The entire troupe was again standing aligned one next to the other on the front of the stage, just behind Sylvestre and Anselme. When both arrived at the front, Sylvestre raised Anselme's hand toward the sky, like two Olympic champions. That gesture drew a thunder of applause. It was done; the message was passed on, and the evening was much more than a success; it was the success of everyone in the stadium. There were even some disabled spectators seated in their wheelchairs, who asked for help from the people around them to stand. So, what was the gift for Anselme.

The immense pride felt by the members of the band, watching

their family with tears in their eyes, was indescribable. All those years, they had to lie to their relatives no longer counted.

To their surprise, the public still wanted more. They invited once more all the stars that had helped them make it happen, to come and play and sing with them, to close the show, with an piece from Dan Year Braz, on the track 'Green Lands'. A general symbiosis settled on that surreal scene on the edge of the supernatural, to the great pleasure of the public.

Thus the unusual concert ended was, which singlehandedly change the lives of millions of people.

The musicians were acclaimed for more than twenty minutes, the reunion with Anselme lasted meanwhile, two long heures. No one could stop talking. It came to a point where Michael felt obliged to stop it spreading by word of mouth the following message:

"I can only guess at what you were feeling, but we must go; a big feast awaits everyone with Anselme as master of ceremonies. It will be for next week, time enough to recover from your emotions. Spread the word... and congratulations. It was really great; well done."

He took the microphone and spoke directly to the ever present public and still under the spell of the show.

'Ladies and gentlemen, no need to ask you if you enjoyed this evening with us! We thank you all for your participation. As much as I also am in the heat of the moment, we have to respect certain commitments such as an event like this requires. Also, I would like to ask you to please head towards the designated exits. Again thank you and take care.'

The climate was still as captivating and enchanting. The public did not object and promptly cooperated. The site emptied in just over half an hour in Michael's amazement. Only musicians and families were still on the scene. The 'stars of the Celtic world,' also present, complimented the members of the 'Troupe Méribell'. The words were not strong enough and lacked adjectives to describe that fabulous evening.

The next day, everyone went home to start their new lives.

Local and national newspapers described a superb evening, outstanding for some, supernatural and majestic for others, or grand, beautiful, miraculous. All the range of synonyms that were similar to or indirectly related to the word 'sublime' had certainly been used that day.

Michael, who had not planned to publish the concert was soon be 'forced' to ask the now famous Troupe and the various stars who had joined them the permission to do it. Troupe Méribell had no intention of going into show-business. But soon, she was nevertheless offered for concert dates in the same spirit everywhere in France and later in Europe.

The future will reveal, that they will accept some, given the importance of their message.

But they will not jump, at any cost, in that hellish life of travel, stress and lack of sleep. The few dates they will do are but proof of their physical achievement, but certainly not a vocation; their greatest wish was to catch up with their families. That will allow them, additionally, to live that adventure and fully appreciate all the rewarding moments. In the heat of the moment, excited by that new life of about one year, some of them will grow twice faster. But all, without exception, now knew what they want to make of their lives; they have come to dream again…

17

Back to basics...

'Do not be afraid to move slowly, but only be afraid of stopping.'
Arthur Schopenhauer

I n both families on the road back to Saint-Just, the atmosphere was serene, with a touch of general excitement. Bernard, Suzanne and Sofia's parents had warmed up to each other and had decided to stay an extra day in the capital.

In Sébastien's car the same musical atmosphere prevailed. Anselme thought all his 'new friends' he had once cared for; he continued to thank them in his thoughts for the great gift they had given him.

When they arrived at the path that lead to their home, they could see Drakkar, overjoyed to see them. Not having seen the car coming, Yannick began a vain pursuit, then understood the pooch's joy. It was obvious that he was not going to calm down.

Anselme went out first and went to meet them.

'Hello, Yannick. Thank you for taking care of the dog.'

Drakkar did not give him the opportunity to say more. He had rushed over him like a charging boar, placing his front paws on his chest, licking his face.

'Congratulations Anselme!' said Yannick.

'Your parents told you about the evening?'

'Yes, they called me that morning, and you've given them quite a show, it seems.'

'There is some truth to that, but it's mostly me who got quite a show!'

'They told me that, too. Anyway, it's great what they did for you. There are even some rumours starting to run in the village.'

'ALREADY!'

'There were some families of musicians who know, and they talk to everyone. See, yesterday they were on wheelchairs and now they bring them around as luggage for the most part!'

'I don't think it's just your imagination, Yannick. But I admit that seeing it all in one night, it was all like a dream.'

'I understand; I leave you to settle in now. See you later!'

'See you later, Yannick, and thank you again.'

'Don't mention it, Anselme.'

He joined the car to help unload the luggage.

'Leave it, Constance, I got it. Greg, Seb, you're staying over tonight, right?'

'Of course, Dad,' replied Sébastien; 'Moreover, we're all exhausted, and I don't think many people would need these old bones tonight!'

With that, the two took their father in their arms.

'We're proud of you, Dad.'

Anselme was able to realise his luck. Against any delay, Grégory had quieted and had evolved in such a way that he commanded life; there was happiness in his eyes as he enjoyed this time, however short it may be, with his father and brother. Anselme was moved by that moment so valuable and unique.

'And you are my pride; I love you my sons.'

While the three boys were playing with Drakkar in the garden, Constance and her two beautiful girls watched them with tenderness.

This precious moment with his sons, threw him into a spiral of emotion he had felt the day before; he had not realised that he held them with all his strength against him, and that he was 'smothering' them already.

'Dad... Dad... we love you too, but we can't breathe!'

Anselme smiled and 'let go'. With still his sharp humour, Grégory turned to his mother.

'Forget the fifty euros... I nearly died of suffocation... Make it at least double!'

Amused, Anselme abounded in jest in a cool and serious manner.

'Well... I leave you three seconds headstart; I suggest that you must be as far away from this house when I get to three!'

It was touching to see that 'young old man,', somewhat boorish and often clumsy, have fun that way, with his children.

'And you Sébastien, you agree, right?'

'Yes, Dad,' he said, 'approaching his brother for protection!'

'So much the worse for you, you asked for it!' He continued, going towards their direction!

The two men began to run like young children, laughing and continuing to tease their father.

'You can still run, you're too old to catch up!'

'That's what you think!' said Anselme, who began to run out of breath.

After two laps around the house, he stopped by the luggage, looking at Constance.

'They're right, I'm done for!

'Keep some energy for the luggage... That's no longer for your age grandpa!'

'What...? You also want me to run after you?'

'You've already done so, a little over forty-five years ago... and you got me... Don't you remember?'

Anselme smiled. He seemed calmer since their return, as if relieved of a burden.

'And how I remember it, dearest!'

'There was a long time since you had not told me...'

'I'm a little distracted, I must've forgotten!'

The rest of the evening took place in the same atmosphere. They finished the evening meal past 10:00 p.m.; time in which everyone showed clear signs of fatigue. Invited over for dinner, Yannick was a real live wire when he wanted to be. He felt at home; he was at ease. It was between dirty jokes that he told some anecdotes on the now famous 'Pretty Bush' but his eyes were beginning to lag behind his enthusiasm; he decided to spend the night at his parents'.

'Thank you for a good evening,' he said, pushing his chair back. 'At this very moment, it looked like it was your forte! I really enjoyed myself in every way. I guess you won't be up long either, so I'll wish you a good night.'

Sébastien. Grégory, their respective wives and children did the same. Constance cleared the table with the help of Anselme who prepared a second coffee accompanied by Italian 'grappa'; a habit he had in Italy during a certain period of his life. He settled on one of the chairs in the garden, contemplating the stars in the sky, as he did regularly after dinner. It relaxed him, allowed him to meditate, as he used to say.

"Fifteen years, they took fifteen years to get there... It's true that, unlike me, they were hit hard, legs and coccyx, that's why, it only took me three years. Hats off to you guys! Definitely next Sunday, we'll be there."

Constance had finished putting everything away. She joined him with a cup of tea in hand and sat on a chair next to him.

'Have they moved since the day before yesterday?' she joked.

'If that was the case, I did not notice! But on the other hand, many other things will move. Since last night, I haven't stopped thinking about, thinking about the future.'

'A penny for your thoughts?'

'I had some insights... you must know, Constance...'

'What?'

'Our experience... What they did, what I did. I wonder if I should get into writing!'

'Do you intend to become a writer?'

'That, I don't know yet, but I want everyone to know. I don't mean the times of suffering, but of the spirit which allows you to achieve such results, you know?'

'Why not, if that's what you want to do. You think a lot of people would be interested to know of your feat?'

'I can't say too much; maybe not the "exploit" in itself, but simply the fact that you get to know yourself better, or discover more about yourself.'

'I can't wait to read you, darling! About reading, we received mail and there was a letter addressed to you, do you want to see it?'

'No, see I don't want to. It's late, you're tired and I only have two wishes; finish my coffee, and go to bed with you.'

'That's a great idea,' confirmed Constance. 'I'll brush my teeth and I'll head upstairs. Don't fall asleep here, I'll be waiting.'

'Don't worry, I'll be with you in ten minutes,' he assured her.

Two minutes went by; he was exhausted and excited at the

same time. But he had more strength; his eyes began to flicker and he gradually fell asleep, with his hot cup of coffee in hand.

Drakkar was lying beside the chair. For him, sleeping outside was not a problem, but for Anselme, it was different. Certainly it was not chilly 'thanks' to his hypertension. But the small eleven degrees that the thermometer displayed were meanwhile conducive in having him catch cold; besides he could easily spill the hot cup of coffee. Dozing off often happened to him. When ended by sleep in the living room, he often spent the entire night there, if not awakened by a noise. But when he slept outside with such freshness, he woke himself, at about two in the morning usually seized by the cold.

Suddenly Drakkar opened one eye and held his ears up. A cat? No… It certainly was not the cold either. After all, he is sled dog, and he can withstand temperatures way lower than that. But, it did not rise to defend the house and his master, for he knew that silhouette that was there, right in front of him. It was not a person of flesh and blood. Its body was not even palpable. It was translucent, slightly hazy; for him, even if he was the only one to see, he was part of the family. Each time he visited, Drakkar was entitled friendly petting. The communication between the two was clear. He was certain that if the figure gave him an order, he would obey him as he would Anselme. But tonight, it preferred to act by itself, as it had done in the Disneyland bar toilet or in many other occasions. So in order to once again avoid the inconvenience of the cool night or that of overturned coffee cup, it put its hand on his shoulder and shook him slightly to wake up.

'Yes, sweetheart I'm coming, sorry for making you wait!' he said, fully asleep.

At that time, he opened his eyes, he saw no one else but Drakkar, but he was not afraid as long; although he did feel that someone had kindly moved his shoulder. And it could not have been Constance, since she would be snoring on the upper floor...

'Thank you" he said, rising and finishing his cup of still warm coffee.

"I'm off to thank all the mist I see up the end of my days!" He thought.

'Come on, Drakkar, let's go...'

Straightening up, the dog looked at him as if he looked at someone and let out one of those little quiet "woo" of which he has the secret. Much to the amazement of Anselme who was watching the scene, the fur on top of his head stood again.

Everything suddenly became clear; there really was someone or rather something; visibly coming to him 'in peace' and to help. Anselme could not see it, but he was apparently able to admit that fact. When he closed the door, he looked at his garden for a moment. At that point, he thought about what he had said to Rémy at the concert, before the great screen. He smiled and went to bed.

The next morning, 7:00 a.m.; Anselme rose, made coffee and was preparing for his daily walk as is his usual. Drakkar knew. Before going out, he went back to ask Constance what he should buy the way, so as not to yell from downstairs.

'Just get some bread, I have everything I need for today.'

Anselme grabbed the leash and began his little journey. "Hi Nanar" he said in passing. There was no change in his habits; that morning more than others. When he arrived near the 'Hotel Méribell' his heart began to beat faster. Today was a new way he looked at the old clinic; he felt pride and joy. A feeling of happiness came over. He was sure of it, something has definitely changed, and it was only the beginning. Since then, he no longer saw just the suffering that he had had once known in those walls, but a victory, that of man. It was in that spirit that he wrote his book. There was no intention of making the reader cry; he must feel the same way as us, 'the desire to be' simply.

18

We finally meet again

'The truth is not in one dream, but in many dreams.'
Jean-Paul Sartre

Back home, he removed the dog's leash, placed the bread on the kitchen table, and headed to the living room where the mail was received during their absence. He took the one personally addressed to him, opened it with a paper cutter, then suddenly turned over to the side where the address was written.

"Bizarre, that stamp... it's still in Francs, as in the year... but... what does it mean..."

His eyes widened suddenly.

'What, nineteen-ninety-four! I'll go tell that postal service!'

But he forgot an essential thing; a secret carefully guarded by a person he never thought of. Nicole, the 'great little woman' with strong character as he had called her, had sent the letter herself. At the time, a Post-It was stapled on it...

'To mail only on 24 December 2013'.

It still took out the letter from the envelope and began to read...

Anselme my friend,

As you saw, everything is possible, but that you already knew that. You will quickly realise that from dream to reality, there is just but one step. I knew I am present in your memories and in your dreams; know that I will always be with you.

The idea of the book is excellent, and I can a thunderous success. Allow me to send you those few words, I hereby grant you the copyright.

'You can think, that to have nothing to do in this world if life has taken away your motor skills; but it's up to you to decide to take it from its place or to be disabled'

Take care of yourself my friend.

"I know some people who would are better off having a leg less!" commented Anselme in thought.

PS: Nicole was the only one who truly knew of our relationship. This is her handwriting and you would perhaps understand better today this decision I made back then; I had to ask her to sign Rémy...

"How I understand you little brother... But, but... what is happening to me?"
He flashed a wide smile, then pulled himself together.
"I knew it... I did not want to admit it, but I suspected it... I should have realized earlier that it was you. I knew I shouldn't be surprised when it comes to you, but how could you know? I knew you had sensory abilities, but now you're just showing off!"
Suddenly Anselme felt a cold draft, behind him. At that time

everyone was still asleep in the house except Constance was eating lunch in the kitchen, he had the feeling of not being alone.

Even if they had been waiting for several days, what he prepared to do somewhat destabilized him because until then, the only spirit which he addressed without speech was that of a living person; but today was going to be a first for him. That was at least what he believed...

For starters, he did not know whether to speak or simply think, or simply just wait. Maybe, would he see the same light he had seen the day before, when he was in the bus, Perhaps, it would materialize in the form of a translucent man like in the movies?

He ventured cautiously in that supernatural contact with a certain resolve.

'Rémy...?' He whispered.

A few seconds passed.

'Rémy, are you there? I am alone now you can show yourself...'

He waited a few moments before continuing his supernatural approach...

'You haven't done all this just to let me down, now I'm ready! I konew you're there... answer...'

Anselme felt at that time, a mixture of impatience, joy, excitement and fear. The letter in his hands, hands behind his back, he waited as an administrative client queuing at a counter to be served.

"What were you waiting for... come on, show yourself!"

A few minutes passed when suddenly...

'You don't have to talk, you know!'

Great happiness settled on his face accompanied by a tear.

"There you are," he thought, "We finally meet again."

'We will communicate as we did before?'

'To begin with, yes. You're not okay with it?'

'Of course I am. Why can I not see you?'

'All in good time, my friend.'

'Where are you?'

'Right next to you, but you can't see me today... Although...'

'Why, I saw you yesterday...'

'Because you really believed it, you felt no fear. Besides, you "Wanted to know me" and possibly help me.'

'That hasn't changed.'

'Quite so, actually, Anselme. You were torn between whether nor not you should believe. Yesterday, you were once again the small child who flew high, and who didn't ask many questions; while today you doubted, you wanted to be sure you were not dreaming. Those are the differences.'

'And that's why I can't see you now?'

'We often see that what we want to believe, especially, that it may be accepted. It was much easier for children because their 'small minds' were not yet polluted by life. If they see, they see and that's it; if an adult sees, he will say at first, it's impossible, I must be dreaming, he will fear.

It's of course, not as simple in all cases, but what one can remember was that the predisposition that all children with these phenomena. A bit like you, with your 'seven-league boots,' when you wandered over the city. And yesterday you had that predisposition, perhaps because you knew it would not be...'

'There has to be that. When I read your letter just now, I thought so strongly and asked myself so many questions, I ended up having cold feet. Do you know that you were the first death with which I "trimmed a bib"!'

'No...'

'For once I taught you something!'

'No... I'm not the first dead you've spoken to.'

136

'What do you mean?

'You have already talked with your dead neighbor; you also played with "Kalinka"... The 'Malamute' sled dog you had when you were a kid, you remember, right?'

'Of course, I remember; how could I forget such moments.'

'When you saw them in your dreams, it was much more than that; you were really with them. That was another form of disembodiment. The precise moment when you played and caressed your dog, or when you chatted with your neighbor, both had just died.'

'That's right, you're right, so you're the third "dead" I've talked to!'

'Not anymore, because there have been others, but you don't remember.'

'Who?'

He changed his mind...

'No, don't tell me, I don't want to knew for now. Now that we're together again, I want to ask you a bunch of questions.'

'Please, Anselme, I'd be happy to answer you.'

'I've always had trouble understanding why you left so soon. I admit that you had virtually no family, but there were at least four people who loved you in this earth, and I was one of them. With the capabilities that you had, surely you could get back up like that Russian paraplegic. To be frank with you, I've always resented the fact that you just gave up. If you knew the emptiness you left; when I came to your room and saw your impeccably empty bed. Actually, I saw again those times when we were chatting. All those jokes you're telling me; I was sure that you'd make it, and sometimes I even imagine us going together at the corner bistro, drink coffee and talk face to face. You did not have the right to leave us like that... I loved you Rémy, you were like a brother to me. So why Rémy… why?'

'I knew it would affect you very much, but I had no choice, it was my moment, I felt deep within me. You should knew that we all have, such as we are, a "Main mission" to accomplish. A mission that still has a direct relation to our own evolution; and that was precisely what I did. My 'normal life' stopped when I had my accident and I should have died that day…'

'Why did you stay then?'

'Can't you guess?'

'I think so, but I'd rather you still tell me.'

'That was for you, Anselme. If you had not known me, you wouldn't have gotten out of your disability, you would have given up, you would become embittered and you would pushed around in a wheelchair today. Okay, sure, you would have still tried, for yourself, as well as for Constance and your children, but the resentment that you would've harboured would've destroyed everything, starting with your marriage. What saw you through, was to have had a friendship with another disabled person like me, who could only move his eyes. In addition, you would have missed your life, because today it's completely changed.'

'That's right, it has changed dramatically! And thinking about it, you gave me more, you gave me the love of a brother. Certainly you I missed you and I'll always do but I got to know that fraternal feeling thanks to you, and then I know now we'll be together again, so to say. But why wait that long to show yourself?'

'I revealed myself almost immediately after my death, but you did not see, or rather you could not see it because it wasn't the right time. You were too disturbed.'

'And when was the right time?'

'When you began to accept my death.'

'I've never really accepted it completely, you know.'

'Oh yes! You started to mourn, not a long time ago, without realizing it, but you did it!'

'Maybe… But then, why was it that I haven't been able hear you or see you, nor even feel you?'

'Think for a moment… If you cannot accept my death, how can you expect to see or hear my mind?'

'Maybe, but we were already doing in your lifetime…'

'But it has nothing to do it! When I lived, you did not need to consider or imagine anything, because I was there. The principle was perhaps the same, but there was a big difference.'

'What was it?

'Do I need to explain everything you to? Besides, you already know the answer…'

'I insist!'

Rémy laughed a good laugh; he was just as happy as Anselme over their reunion somewhere ordained by destiny.

'You'll never change… The difference comes naturally; when you're dead, we no longer have a physical body, therefore no more "earthly presence," and that's where faith comes into play; you can't see and hear that if you have faith in what you see. It may be unrealistic to expect that it to be easy to make the difference in a world where visual deceptions aided by current technology can easily fool our eyes, but it's possible. You must have the same purity as children. Do you understand?'

'And that's what's happening to me then?'

'Precisely, Anselme! In your case, given your age, you may call that wisdom…'

'So you're telling me that you were always by my side, though I suspected nothing!'

'Ever since…'

'So, death is nothing, in the end!'

'No, it was just one step in our earthly and spiritual life. The hardest in death, is the loneliness and emptiness it creates for those who remain, as well as seeing loved ones suffer, for those who leave. I admit I had a lot of trouble to see you sad as well, but you had to experience it to know the difference.'

Throughout the conversation, Anselme began to distinguish a white aura before him; he was beginning to see...

The face of Anselme lit up, beaming in wonder.

'I... I think I see you...

'You see, when you want to!'

Physically alone in the room, Anselme began to laugh; it aroused Constance's curiosity who soon came to join him. Arriving in the living room, she saw her husband laughing, as if someone had told him a joke.

She approached him to give him a kiss.

'Hello my angel,' Anselme said cheerfully.

'Hello my dear heart, what is happening to you, I heard you in the kitchen?'

'Should I tell her?' he thought, taking care to hide the letter.

'No, no, wait for a moment. For now, it's better to avoid unnecessary hassle.'

Anselme returned Constance's kiss.

'It's okay honey, I just remembered something funny...'

Me, rebuilding my life... with you!

'You seem to me... I don't know how to say... Much better, changed...'

He observed her for a few seconds and looked in her eyes, giving her another kiss, while gently brushing her hair back in place with his fingers.

'Now yes... I'm much better...'

Constance jumped in the same direction, and then pulled

140

herself together.

'Would you like another coffee?'

'Yes, I do… Give me five minutes and I'll be there.'

'I'll have it ready.'

She went back into the kitchen, while Anselme resumed his conversation with Rémy.

'You love like it's the first time, it's touching!'

'Forgive me for not picking up on that, but I have other questions.'

'I'm listening.'

'The fact that I can distinguish your aura, does it make me someone "Pure"?'

'In a way, yes, it's the light that you see when you die. But you can never be "pure" as you say; all in all least not in this world…'

'Of course; you speak of that same light which those who are clinically dead for a few minutes speak of?'

'You really want to know?'

Anselme had a moment of hesitation.

'After all, it's not so important, I saw you again, and that's what matters.'

'That was wise… For your information, know that death is not an end but a continuation… you'll see for yourself, and I'll be there to guide you. Now you'd better go find your one and only, she might get impatient.

'As for me, I'll be back. I look forward to our reunion, and to our little "soul to soul." Chat. See you soon my friend.'

Drakkar did his little friendly "woo": "goodbye Rémy."

'And you knew from the beginning, didn't you?' said Anselme watching his dog.

Rémy gave the animal a pat on its head, and then went off as fast as light.

Still holding the letter in his hands, he looked up, slowly scanned the room around him, and nodded his agreement. He now knew he would have by his side a ghost, a friend, "in life as in death" outside of these fantastical reunions, he could now live his life and fulfill his destiny, until he himself should comply with the order of resounding 'post-life' recreation and thus join his great friend in a world where mistakes in life turn into lessons and similar experiments are used to climb the first step of the staircase that leads to the repose of the soul.

At that moment, he had a sense of déjà vu, as if he had experienced that in a premonitory dream...

Epilogue

'I feel neither sorry for the past, nor do I fear the future.'
Ernest Renan

Anselme developed his relationship with Rémy little by little, that he admitted the reality of his presence in his life. He distinguished it better and better, to be able to grasp the features of his face – at least, those he knew of. Now they communicate by words in his dreams... this time with a nuance.... he will remember it as an enlightened conversation. They will refine their same telepathic abilities and will continue to philosophy as they did in the past. Being aware of the situation of Constance was no longer surprised to see her husband talking and laughing alone.

In the same manner, she became accustomed to the pranks that the two friends would pull; for example, look at an object to rise in the air pretending to control it remotely, with his hands.

Constance will go through three successive stages, fear, habit, then tiredness quickly set in; to the point where when she wanted to talk to Anselme, she was forced to take certain precautions...

'Anselme, where were you?'

'Here in the garden.'

'I'd like to talk to you...'

'I'm listening, my angel...'

'Alone... !'

"I'll be going now, Anselme!"

"Yes, scram! She's in a bad mood today!'

There, an air current would move away, and Constance would only say, "Thank you".

Early in their new relationship, Anselme and Rémy had fun like two unruly children... They were such demons!

Anselme went from discovery to discovery. Rémy told him among other things, what he needed to know about life, death... He would eventually be so comfortable on the sofa of his brain, he developed two additional capacities, 'wisdom' and 'love'.

Then, having gained confidence, he wrote his book and will have it published a year and a half later.

He will talk about his own experience and that of the members of Troupe Méribell that will contribute to the writing of the book. He would also discuss what he considered the good and the bad sides of technological progress, without being too biased. Finally, he will develop in detail, the ability to tap into one's deepest self, energy and motivation necessary for healing and remission from illness or disability, still today considered incurable and irreversible, concluding with the phrase:

"As long as we remain convinced that all is lost, it cannot be otherwise."

That will cause strong reactions in some people born with a disability, whose muscles have atrophied and have not had the opportunity to make a difference.

At the beginning of the publication of his book, Anselme will even deal with people from outside his home asking for a miracle; although it will take all the time to explain that miracle, the truth, that it was them.

Thus, he created with the support of his friends the 'Rémy Foundation', which will be largely funded by the dividend his writings to start, then more and more through numerous donations over time. Staying there were men and women who learn much more than to drive a wheelchair... the expanded their autonomy.

It will be understood that the solution can only come from them and them alone; the task was not easy and the damage that can be more or less significant, some will come out standing and others sitting but mentally changed for most. People with "serious" diseases will join the association.

Anselme will in turn be taken very seriously by some, and utopian by others, including the medical profession despite many positive results.

It will give rise to two types of people, those who admit it and others...

Thanks

To all the medical professionals I questioned without respite, during visits to the hospital or to my osteopath and many others I forget. All have helped me, each in their own way to develop the 'technical' aspect of the story.

To all my relatives who never doubted for a moment of my ability to get into such an adventure, because I always 'jot' but I've never had the intention of writing a novel.

As Stephen King said, 'Jotter one day, jot them until the end.'

To my dear and loving wife who uses a lot better than me an azerty keyboard and who encoded the greater part of the words of that manuscript I wrote with a good old pen.

To my boss, who despite some awkwardness I was able to allow me to commit to my work during the writing of this story, having oftentimes been 'elsewhere'. He has demonstrated exemplary patience and kept his confidence in my capability as a driver.

There is also a loyal friend, or should I say, an ally for all times, who guide my life somewhere nine hours a day... I mean the steering wheel of the truck I ride every day and which I use as a desk after work. It's over this improvised and tinkered support that I create the characters who end up taking over my imagination, continuing their own history. As has become a pleasure my nightly breaks.

In conclusion, I dedicate novel to my wife who, not satisfied of having gotten up today was sure to find all those capabilities; I could have drawn my inspiration from her, if I had not written this story two years sooner, but with great fictionalized parts and I recently changed the dates. 'The one who has to live survives even if you the crush them in a mortar.'

That said, we have crossed paths with no ghosts to date!

And finally, to life for simply for being presented to me as it has done with its ups and downs, and above all, for having me meet people at once magical and saving; I was able to open my eyes to many things, mostly about myself...

'The hardest thing when a loved one dies is not going to the cemetery, but going back to it.'
MM.

To bring you to the peak of the 'strong emotions' of the end of the novel, I was listening to the the album, "LA NUIT CELTIQUE" (Stade de France, 15 March 2002 – Sony Music) as I wrote that part.

Therefore, I recommend that after reading, to listen to the following songs in this order starting from chapter 16 of page 135:

No. 1-15-3-5-9-8-6-12

But with a bit of imagination, it might as well be the "sound-track" of the entire novel.

www.ingramcontent.com/pod-product-compliance
Lightning Source LLC
Chambersburg PA
CBHW060122260626
47160CB00005B/1978